ISBN-10: 1547005386

www.theonlyfredsmith.com

Cover art and design by the incomparable Susan Jones.

THE CLOSET

STORIES

FRED SMITH

Also by Fred Smith

The Incident Last Tuesday: a play

Invisible Innocence: my story as a homeless youth
with Maria Fabian

Visit Fred's site **TheOnlyFredSmith.com**

and sign up to his blog

'A Crack in the Room Tone'

to receive his latest stories, movies, and occasional drum solos.

For Marie.

Midnight Blues

"Midnight Blues. You got Mamie."

"Hi. Uh, is this Mamie?" Mamie couldn't help but grin at the familiar sound of a twenty-first-century caller in shock that he'd actually reached not only a live human being at a radio station but the host of the show that was currently on the air.

"Live and loud, sweetie."

"Wow. Cool. We uh…we really missed you." The wavering voice was young.

"Thank you, sweetie. That means a lot. What can I play for you?"

"Listen, Mamie, I just want to say that uh...well I mean, it's not like I know you, but I'm really sorry for…you know, your loss."

Mamie knew the polite thing to do was hold the moment and let the space that hung between her and the unknown caller build with silence, just to the point of being uncomfortable. Her husband deserved that. Her son did, too. But she couldn't bear the thought of breaking down on air and instead took a drag from her cigarette and quickly fired back.

"Thank you, sweetie. How about some Muddy Waters to carry us both to the other side?"

"That would…yeah. Muddy Waters is cool."

"We'll do 'Forty Days and Forty Nights' real soon. Thanks for listening."

She pushed the button that dumped the call then brought on the next.

"Midnight Blues. You got Mamie."

"We love you, Mamie. We're so glad you're back." This voice was female and experienced.

"Thank you, sweetie. It's good to be back."

"I don't even have a request. Everything you play is great. I love the stories you tell about each song, especially the one for the last song of the night. I stay up for that one."

"I do it for you, sweetie, and we'll spin a few words about Willie Dixon this hour. Thanks for listening."

Another drag from her smoke. Another caller.

"Midnight Blues. You got Mamie."

"Mamie, I've been a fan of the show for years. I'm a long time listener…"

"And a first-time caller?" She normally refrained from finishing her caller's sentence, even when it was obvious.

"Guilty as charged."

"What's your name, sweetie?" Mamie wasn't playing favorites. She had long since made a habit of asking the name of every third caller.

"Frank. And I gotta say, I dig that you still spin vinyl on the air. Nothing like a good record."

"It's the only way I know and the only way I go, sweetie. Thanks for calling, Frank. What can I play to set the midnight mood?"

"Well, in honor of your return to the air, how about some Mamie Smith? Let's get back to the roots of the blues."

"Someone's been doing his homework."

"You told the story two years ago," Frank said. "Your mom had just passed away and you told us about how she named you after the first African American to make a blues recording. The year was…oh, I wanna say 1920."

"And what was the song?" Mamie's voice held a certain playful tone as she hoped her question would steer Frank toward blues trivia and away from the painful memory of her mother.

"'Crazy Blues.' Perry Bedford."

"I am impressed, Frank. We'll roll that song this hour. Thanks for listening."

"Thanks for coming back, Mamie. I can only imagine how tough this last year has been for you."

Mamie paused to gather herself.

"Your support means a lot, Frank. Thanks for listening."

She dumped the call, stamped the first Kool of the night in the ashtray next to console, and leaned into the mic.

"You're listening to Midnight Blues on WMLN. I'm your host, Mamie Rogers and for the next hour I'll be taking your requests, so reach out to me the old fashioned way, 'cuz the only social network I know how to work holds court in a bar that still lets you smoke. So let's blaze up the first hour of the show with this little joint from the 1970 movie *Chicago Blues*. It's the live version of 'The First Time I Met The Blues' by Mr. George 'Buddy' Guy."

Mamie closed her eyes and let the piercing guitar licks fill the room. Her nerves had steadied, the way they usually did when Buddy Guy was in her ears. She opened her eyes and found the framed picture of her family next to the mixing console just as the pioneering bluesman howled into the microphone.

The first time I met the blues…

Had it really been a year? Her fans had missed her, at least the ones who cared enough to call in did. They meant well. Harmless and clueless, but they meant well.

Mamie had spent half of the time since her last broadcast trying to convince herself that Jerome and Darren would have wanted her to keep the show going. She spent the other half trying to convince herself she had nothing to do with the accident that took her husband and only son. It was pure coincidence. Did she really believe it? When she was sober she did. The more she drank the more she wondered if her playing the song really did have something to do with it. She wasn't with her family when their car hydroplaned from its lane and crashed head on into another vehicle. She was in this very studio, closing her show with a song she'll forever associate with tragedy.

As Buddy Guy wrapped up the first tune of the evening, Mamie stamped out her cigarette and spoke into the mic.

"From the 1970 documentary *Chicago Blues* directed by Harley Cokeliss, that was Buddy Guy with my favorite version of 'The First Time I Met the Blues.' The film offered a look into the working-class lives of the windy city's bluesmen and presented a portrait of struggle, inequality, and the will of artistic spirit to explain it all as the blues has done for the American Negro since the days of the spiritual hymn." Mamie paused to light another smoke.

"A lot of you have called in to extend your condolences. If we were all in the same bar, the next round would be on me." Another toke. Another cloud exhaled.

"I've tried to explain a lot to myself in the year I've been away from this show. And any answers I've found point back to me being right here leaning over the mic with a Kool in one hand and the next record in the other. I can't explain why we suffer the way we do any better than you can. All we can do is lament and keep moving. So let's move on with a man from Mississippi who grew up to become *the* man many consider to be the father of modern Chicago Blues. Recorded on the Chess label in 1956, here is Muddy Waters with 'Forty Days and Forty Nights.'"

Mamie dropped the needle and closed her eyes as the song's opening vocals shook the studio walls.

Forty days…and forty nights…since my baby left this town.

She opened her eyes and locked them on her husband in the picture next to the console.

Sun shinin' all day long…but the rain keep coming down.

Jeromes eyes held a mystery that Mamie had always taken great joy in realizing wasn't hers to completely decipher. Sometimes they could be playful. Other times they were romantic. When the world was particularly harsh they could be cut from stone. But in this moment, the moment Mamie had chosen to carry her through the first broadcast since the accident, they were warm.

The picture she'd framed and placed on the mixing console had been taken about a week before the accident. Seconds before it was snapped, she and Jerome had been arguing about bills, taxes owed, and a financial future that was turning bleaker every year. They'd let their voices carry through the house, which was out of character for the couple. Darren made his entrance as the spat reached fever pitch. The boy slid into his father's arms, held out Mamie's phone and snapped a selfie of he and his dad, the both of them looking like everything was right in the world. That was the moment Mamie had chosen to carry her through her first night back on the air.

She's my life I need her so…and why she left I just don't know.

She lost herself in the song, her thoughts drifting in cadence with the groove, dancing with the guitar licks and harmonica howls. The glowing call light broke Mamie from her trance. As Muddy Waters closed out his song, she leaned into the mic.

"That was Muddy Waters with a 'Forty Days and Forty Nights', recorded in 1956 on the Chess Label. It spent six weeks on the Billboard R&B chart where it peaked at number seven. Two years earlier, Waters recorded another hit for producer Leonard Chess in 'Hoochie Coochie Man.' The song reached number eight on Billboard's Black Singles chart and, in addition to being inducted into the Blues Hall of Fame in 1984, it was voted number two-twenty-seven on Rolling Stone's list of the five hundred greatest songs of all time.

"Let's take another call. Midnight Blues. You got Mamie."

The line was silent.

"Don't be shy, sweetie. What's on your mind?" A crash of thunder rumbled overhead. Mamie could feel the summer rain begin to pound the studio from above. She reached for the call dump button.

"Last chance," she said in a tone that was anything but threatening.

"This show means a lot to me," said a thin and crackling voice.

"Thank you, sweetie. Means a lot to me, too. What can I play for you as the Saturday night storm rolls in?"

"I've got a request."

"That's what we do, sweetie. Lay it on me."

"I want you to play," the voice paused as if the next words were the bridge leading to the guitar solo, "I want you to play 'Let Me Hold You' by Audrey Jackson."

A crash of thunder shook the room. Mamie held her silence.

One year ago to the day, she had closed her show with this little-known tune from a diva who, along with her lover and co-songwriter, died when she was not yet nineteen. Miles from the WMLN studio that same night, two more young souls were leaving this world before their time. Jerome and Darren's tickets had been punched sometime while "Let Me Hold You" played across the local airwaves. Out of respect for her departed family, Mamie had made the promise to never play this song again—to never mention it again, much less listen to it.

"I've retired that song from the show, sweetie. Personal reasons. But maybe a little Billie Holiday will tame what ails you."

"I understand your aversion," the voice was steady despite its lo-fi timbre, "but 'Let Me Hold You' is a very important song for me, you see. It was the last song my wife and I listened to before she left me."

Mamie was silent.

"And I'd like very much for you to find it in your heart to play it because I want it to be the last song I hear before I die."

Dump the call.

Every instinct Mamie had told her to dump the call and hit the delay button. If you do it now, you can cover over the caller's statement. It may be a jarring cut for the audience, but she could always claim the storm had caused a bit of technical difficulty.

Mamie kept the call live and waited for the man to explain himself. When he didn't, she prodded his enigmatic request.

"I'm not sure I follow, mister. Are you sick?"

"Of the body, no. Of the heart, I'm afraid so."

Mamie considered his response, then prodded further.

"I'm still not sure I-"

"I'm going to kill myself. Tonight. I'm going to end my life, and I'd like to do it after listening to 'Let Me Hold You' by Audrey Jackson."

Mamie pushed the delay and hold buttons simultaneously. The call was off the air and waiting to resume. Mamie prayed she had hit the delay button in time to spare the listening audience of the caller's plans, assuming she heard them right.

The caller's voice hadn't wavered when he revealed his intention and Mamie couldn't discern whether his threat was genuine. She looked around the studio and was suddenly unnerved that she was alone.

She leaned to the mic.

"Our last caller with the broken heart seems to have hung up on us," Mamie said. "Guess we have a bit of a prankster staying up with us tonight. It's all good. Let's keep the show going. 'Hoochie Coochie Man' was written by the legendary Willie

Dixon who, along with Muddy Waters, has been called the most influential hand in shaping the post-World War II Chicago blues sound. From 1959 here is Willie Dixon with 'Built for Comfort' on WMLN's Midnight Blues."

Mamie looked at her family, took a deep breath, then clicked back to the call.

"Hello?" she said. "Are you still there?"

"You lied to them, Mamie. Said I was a joker. I'm not joking."

"It sounded like the conversation was getting a bit heavy for the air."

"Don't mean to be overly-dramatic, Mamie. I thought you liked it when your callers opened up to you on the air. Isn't that your thing?"

"Sometimes, hearing a person tell me about the blues helps me find the right song for the moment."

"You're a soulful version of Delilah. And you play better music."

"Thanks. I try. Now, I seem to remember you saying—."

"I said was I was going to kill myself and wanted to hear a special song when I did."

"Why would you want to do that, mister?"

"It's a helluva song, Mamie. You have to admit."

"You know that's not what I meant."

"Why does anyone take his own life, Mamie? The mere thought of going on becomes too much to bear. Death presents itself as the only viable option."

"And you figured my show was the place to let the world know you were ready to step off?"

"It'll all make sense soon enough, Mamie. But don't worry about your audience getting sentimental over me. You hit the delay button in time. They didn't hear a thing. It's just you and me, off the air."

"What is your name, sir?" In the immediate wake of the circumstances, Mamie decided her rule of thirds in asking callers their names would be temporarily suspended.

"Does it matter?"

"I wouldn't have asked if it didn't."

"Very well. If my identity is so important to you, call me… Willie."

"That's not your real name." Mamie maintained as non-threatening a tone as she could.

"No, it's not. But it is an apt moniker, given I won't be here much longer."

"Ok then, *Willie*," Mamie continued. Pushing a suicidal caller was a tact whose chances for a successful outcome were statistically limited. She tried to stay polite. "I have to change the record right now. Promise me you won't kill yourself while I'm gone, OK?"

"Not until I hear my request," Willie said with a light chuckle.

Mamie put the call on hold and got on the mic.

She kept her eye on the blinking light above the console, which indicated her suicidal caller was still on hold. *Stay there, Willie. Stay there.* She took an extra few seconds to compose herself and suppress the sense of panic that was brewing in her voice.

"Let's keep the mood rolling with another legendary Willie in blues history. Released in 1930 on the Columbia label, this is Blind Willie Johnson with 'Trouble Will Soon be Over.'"

The light was still blinking. For a moment Mamie considered calling 9-1-1, then she clicked back to the call.

"Still there, Willie?"

"For now."

"Good. I figured since you called me to announce that you were going to kill yourself, you wouldn't mind chatting for at least a few minutes."

"If it pleases you."

"I'm a sucker for good conversation, Willie." Mamie stamped out her cigarette and promptly lit another.

"You really shouldn't smoke, Mamie."

"Health tips from a guy with a death wish." Mamie blew a cloud of smoke and wondered if she had pushed too far. "But enough about me. You a bluesman, Willie?"

"Not particularly."

"Then how'd you end up such a fan of this show?"

"A fortunate stroke of serendipity. One year ago to the day, my wife and I were driving home and came across Midnight

Blues. We have one of those satellite radios in the car, but we both prefer the idea of a neighborhood voice selecting the songs that are broadcast through the air. And I have to say, we were both drawn to your voice and the stories you tell. You're very good, Mamie. I love that you actually play records over the radio. Everything is so damn digital now, don't you think? It's nice to know someone out there still feels the need to touch something real."

"I'm feeling you, Willie. And you're right. Truth is I built up such a collection of vinyl over the years that trying to transfer it to digital seemed like colorizing *The Defiant Ones*. Just because we can doesn't mean we should. Am I right?

"You are."

"Can't help how I feel, Willie. Can we talk about your wife?"

"Why not? She's the reason I'm doing this."

Mamie took a drag of her cigarette, a stalling tactic that gave her just enough time to plot her line of questioning.

"What's her name?"

"Catherine."

"And I can tell you love her."

"More than anything in this world."

"How does she feel about you, Willie?"

"Oh, I'm sure she still loves me too. Wherever she is."

"Where is she, Willie?"

"She died."

Mamie's stomach tightened. How many times in the last year had she been on Willie's end of this conversation? How many times had casual acquaintances, trying to make harmless small talk, forced Mamie to reveal her trampled soul? *I'm so sorry, Mamie. I had no idea. How did it — Is there anything I can do?*

"I'm sorry, Willie. How long were you married?"

"Thirty-six years," Willie answered. "We met in high school."

"Wow. You don't see that much these days."

"No, I suppose you don't."

"Any kids?"

"We had a son. He died of a pulmonary infection when he was two and a half."

"Jesus, Willie. I'm sorry."

"It was a long time ago. I've made my peace."

"Still, no good man deserves to suffer like that."

"What makes you so sure I'm good?"

"It's in your voice. I'm no shrink, but I've had a lot of voices on the line over the years and I can tell that yours is good. You're a good person, Willie."

"There's no one left."

"I'm sorry?"

"I have no family. That's what you were getting at. You wanted to see if I'd be leaving anyone behind when I killed myself. That's why you asked if I have kids. Well, I don't. I'm completely alone."

"It's not easy being alone, Willie. I know. I know about the kind of loss you've been living with and the pain it's caused you. Believe me, I know, Willie."

"Tell me about it," Willie sighed the relaxing sigh of a child waiting for a bedtime story.

"Will it make you change your mind? About killing yourself?"

"I can't make any promises."

"Fair enough. Sit tight while I change the record and I'll tell you all about the blues."

Mamie put the call on hold and leaned into the mic.

"Willie Dixon wrote more than five hundred songs that have been recorded by artists such as Eric Burdon and the Animals, The Rolling Stones, Led Zeppelin, and Phish. None of whom were born when this next artist sold his soul to the devil in a midnight exchange at a cross road in the Mississippi Delta. Recorded in the Gunter Hotel in San Antonio, Texas in 1936, here is Robert Johnson with "Cross Road Blues.""

She clicked back to the phone line.

"Interesting choice," Willie said calmly, "given the circumstances."

"Legend has it Johnson was poisoned," Mamie replied.

"I aways thought the devil came to collect," Willie said.

"Two years after recording this song, Johnson was playing a juke joint on the outskirts of Greenwood, Mississippi. He was offered a drink from a bottle of whiskey by a woman he'd never met. Sonny Boy Williamson tried to dissuade him from partaking, but Johnson replied 'Don't ever knock a bottle out of my hand.' Three days later he was dead. Some say he was poisoned by the juke joint owner, who didn't take too kindly to Johnson's flirting with his wife."

Willie said, "Who's to say it wasn't Lucifer coming to collect? The devil works in mysterious ways. Isn't that what the blues is about? Loss? Speaking of which, you were going to tell me about suffering."

"I know you're in pain, Willie."

"You know what I've told you. What do you know about pain, Mamie?"

"I've lost, Willie. I have." Mamie took a deep breath, knowing she was about to tell a story she had promised to keep for herself.

"I lost my family. My husband. My son. It was a year ago today. I was on the air, and they were coming home. It was a stormy night, just like tonight. They lost control, went into the other lane and hit a car head on. Everyone died. Everyone. I got the call just after I wrapped the show."

"How did it feel when you found out that they were gone?"

Mamie had promised to keep this pain locked inside Until now, she wasn't sure anyone deserved to understand.

"Surreal," she answered. "Like it can't be happening. But I went to the scene. I saw the ambulances. The gurneys carrying death with sheets over them to shield the living from the sight. I had to know. I had to see. And when I uncovered the bodies and saw the blood on my family, I dropped to my knees and screamed."

"Losing a child is something no parent should ever experience," Willie said with a consoling tone that made Mamie relax. "And yet here we are."

"Guess we have something in common, Willie."

"Maybe we do. Have you ever thought of killing yourself, Mamie?"

The thought of ending her own life had staggered through Mamie's mind every night for the last year. Her only remedy against the anguish of suicide's temptation was the bottle, a refuge she sought on a nightly basis—sometimes daily. She needed a drink and pulled out the flask she had decided at the outset of the evening would remain alone until the conclusion of the show. Willie's stinging question convinced Mamie that her plan to maintain professional sobriety was in need of immediate revision. She knew what her tormented caller was going through. Willie had lost the part of his life that kept him going. He'd asked an honest question and deserved the truth. Mamie obliged.

"Yeah, I've thought about suicide," she said as she opened the flask and took in the toxic fumes that smelled of seduction. "I've thought about it a lot over the last year. I almost did it last April. It was Darren's birthday. My boy would have been eleven. I'm one of those moms in mourning who keeps the kid's room exactly how it was.

"On the day of his birthday, I crawled into Darren's bed with a bottle of Jack and a fistful of pills. When I woke up the bottle was gone and the pills were spread out on the floor next to the bed. Guess you could say the booze saved my life that night."

She took a pull from the flask. The first drink always comes with an uneasy combination of guilt and relief. Usually, it took about half the bottle for the guilt to subside, but not tonight. The outside storm unleashed a low rumble of thunder to let the night know it was still up for a dance.

"What brought you back to the air, Mamie?"

"I couldn't live with myself anymore. For a year I've been inside a bottle, numbing my soul from day to dark. I've replayed every moment of that night's show. Based on the time of death in the police report, I know exactly when they died. I know it was just at the end of 'Let Me Hold You' by Audrey Jackson. That's why I can't play that song for you, Willie. It's too painful. It's too soon. I can't bring myself to unearth that heartache. Please understand I can't listen to that song ever again."

"What about the other car in the accident?"

"What about them?"

"You said your husband, what was his name?"

"Jerome."

"Jerome lost control and veered into the other lane."

"That's right," Mamie interjected with a hint of defensiveness. "It was storming and his car hydroplaned. He lost control."

"And here was another car, weathering the same storm. All of the sudden they're slammed by an oncoming motorist. Lives are lost. What have you considered of the other victims?"

"I see her face every night before I go to sleep," Mamie said in a near whisper.

"You see whose face?"

Mamie paused and sparked up another cigarette.

"Got to change the record, Willie. Sit tight."

She jockeyed the next seventy-eight into place and brought her lips to within an inch of the mic. "Sixteen years before Robert Johnson sold his soul at the crossroads, a Vaudeville singer from Cincinnati made history with the first blues recording ever issued. The year was 1920. The label was Okeh and the song was 'Crazy Blues' written by Perry Bradford and performed by Mamie Smith and her Jazz Hounds. This one is for the purists and the historians out there. You know who you are."

She clicked back to Willie.

"Whose face do you see?" he asked calmly.

Mamie closed her eyes and tried to breathe easy, a calming ritual whose intention was not to picture the visage that haunted her each night, but to shake it from her mind's projector. It was no use.

The night of the tragedy, Mamie ran to the second car as the fire department pried its battered shell apart with the jaws of life. The body came next, a woman Mamie could tell was in her fifties, pulled from the passenger side of the wreckage as a matter of course. Mamie knew she should look away, but couldn't. If morbid curiosity had a volume knob, hers was cranked to eleven. Then she saw the face, bloodied but otherwise intact. The woman's eyes were open, forever suspended in the horror of the last moment she would ever know.

Mamie locked on to the victim's perished stare and held a one-way gaze for what felt like an eternity. The woman didn't look scared. She looked surprised, as though she'd just caught a glimpse of an old friend who'd dropped by unannounced. It was then when Mamie noticed the shard of glass protruding from her temple.

What was she thinking about in the moments before the end? Her family, perhaps? Clearly, she was old enough to have a young grandchild. Wouldn't that be a worthy last use of the brain's abilities? What would the child be told the next time he asked about his grandma? The thought always gave Mamie the sensation of being jabbed in the head with an ice pick.

There was a driver, also dead on impact. His body, Mamie could see upon glancing into the mutilated car, was completely upright in the driver seat. His eyes were closed. Thank mercy, Mamie thought. His eyes were closed.

She wished she had never been so curious. She wished she could expunge the victims in the other car from her memory. But they'd become permanent cerebral residents who paid their rent in torment. Whenever Mamie tried to imagine her family, she'd first see this battered pair of strangers.

"Mamie," Willie said, "Whose face did you see?"

"Jesus, Willie I can't. I can't. Please don't make me talk about it."

"It's too painful?"

"Far too painful, Willie. I just can't."

"I understand, Mamie. I do. You don't have to talk about it. Take another drink from the crutch you've got there in the studio and let me do the talking for a bit. You see, I didn't call you tonight as a cry for help. I called you to request a song that is very important to me. 'Let Me Hold You' is important to both of us, Mamie. And the truth is, you and I have a lot more in common than the fact that we've both lost people who were close to us and have considered taking our own lives because if it."

Mamie filled the silence by taking a hearty pull from her flask and stamping her cigarette like it owed her something. When the silence was too much to bear, she broke it with a question of her own.

"What are you saying, Willie?" The storm began to intensify. Mamie lit another smoke.

"The woman you saw, the one whose face haunts you at night, the one whose horror is so ingrained in your mind you'd rather drink yourself to death than press on. She was my wife."

Mamie was silent, stunned. Who was this man? He must be lying. A freak looking for attention. A sadist out for his kinks on a Saturday night. She took another swig from the flask and locked her gaze onto the picture of her family. Her hand fluttered above the call dump button. Then she had a sobering thought.

What if he wasn't lying?

"Mamie?" Willie's voice was calm, but Mamie knew she couldn't answer. Not yet anyway. Not until she could regain her mental bearings and make sense of the mayhem that the conversation had produced. "Mamie?" his voice gained a hint of urgency and now sounded like a parent trying to break a child from a daydream.

"Mamie, you've got dead air."

She snapped back to reality and realized "Crazy Blues" was spinning to the tune of silence, having ended while Mamie was in the throes of Willie's testimony. She fumbled for another record and blindly cued "I Can't Quit You Baby" by Willie Dixon, realizing its title only after the howling vocals of the Chicago bluesman took center stage. How long had she allowed the air to be dead?

"Mamie?"

"Your wife was in the other car?"

"From my perspective, Mamie, it was *your* family who was in the *other* car. But yes she was. That accident, you see, has played a heavy hand in the fate of both of our lives."

"Who was driving?" Mamie tried to remain calm despite feeling the tingle in her hands she knew would soon lead to trembling followed by uncontrollable shaking.

"I was. We were on our way home. From where hardly matters now."

"I thought…I thought the driver was killed."

"Rumors of my death, Mamie. Forgive me if I'm not very good at delivering cliches."

"But I saw…"

"I was unconscious, and may very well have appeared dead, but I can assure you that I was very much alive and remained in a coma for seventeen days. When I came to, I was in a body cast. Broken legs, ribs, back, jaw and a detached retina for good measure. None compared to the pain of realizing my beloved had passed from the event that left me in traction."

Willie paused to let the story sink in. Mamie knew it was her turn to speak, yet could only muster a single word: "Jesus."

"I asked for him too and promptly realized from his silence that I was on my own. There I was, Mamie, laid up in a hospital bed for ten months with no other course but to play the moments before impact in my mind again and again. Every detail of every second. Right up until the headlights of the oncoming car hopped into our lane and collided with our destiny. And what stands out the most? What's so clear is the song: 'Let Me Hold You' by Audrey Jackson. All I knew about the song I learned from the story you told just before playing it. Riveting that I can practically hear it word for word, even now. You're very good, Mamie."

"It doesn't have to be like this, Willie." Mamie could feel her eyes welling. She took a shallow pull from the flask hoping to extract an extra ounce of bravado.

"Unfortunately, it does." Willie's voice was calm. He was determined.

"How are you going to do it?" Mamie asked with a hint of defiance. If sympathy was to have no effect on the caller, maybe shame would.

"I've got a 9 millimeter on my lap. After the song plays. I'm going to put it in my throat and pull the trigger."

Mamie pictured the scene and imagined Willie as she thought he might look. Sitting alone in his living room with a gun in his hand. She saw him taking his life in the manner he had described, the pop of the weapon as the back of his head explodes onto a family portrait. It wasn't right.

"You're lying, Willie."

"Am I?"

"You're not the gun-wielding type."

"What makes you say that?"

"Instinct. I've developed an ear for the truth over these phone lines the last few years. Even if you did own a gun, I don't think you'd turn it on yourself. It's not your style. There's too much that could go wrong. I knew a guy a few years back who tried to do himself through the mouth. Just as he pulled the trigger he jerked his hand and shot a hole through his neck. Should have paralyzed himself, but the dumb son of a bitch lived. Course he's developed a bit of speech impediment since then."

"I'm afraid you've got me pegged, Mamie. I could never shoot myself."

"It's not worth it, Willie. I know you're hurting. And Lord knows, so am I. But I will stay on this line for as long as it takes until you realize that people like you and me, we're survivors of something most people will never understand. We were meant to live and show people what it means to be strong."

"You're quite the preacher, Mamie. Does it run in the family?"

"Is it that obvious?"

"I imagined you might be a preacher's daughter. The studio is your altar and your listeners are your flock."

"My daddy didn't have much use for the blues," Mamie confessed. "Said it was the devil's music that kept our people down. He never understood that it's what's gotten us through since the days of slavery."

"He still alive?" Willie's voice had taken on an even greater sense of calm.

"He died when I was eighteen," Mamie said, taking another hearty pull from her flask as she shuffled the next record into place. "Last thing I ever said to him probably did him in. I told him that we don't know if there is a God, but Muddy Waters is playing the 708 Club in Chicago so that's where I'm going. I left home and I never saw him again."

Telling a stranger about her father had, to Mamie's surprise, a soul-cleansing effect. She recalled the night of his funeral, when she returned to the house she grew up in, now dark and lifeless. She remembers the creak of the living room floor as she walked across it, trying to channel the good times her family had enjoyed together, but all she could feel was the angst that had driven her to rush out into the world she was learning was every bit as harsh as Muddy Waters and friends suggested.

Jerome was with her that night. Without saying a word, he stepped to the center of the living room as the first notes of "Let Me Hold You" rang through her dad's record player. She remembers how the moonlight sneaked through the window and splashed Jerome's young body. His eyes glinted with strength and protection as she buried herself in his arms and they danced slowly as Audrey Jackson emoted her song that, in that moment, seemed to have been written just for them.

It was a memory she kept just for herself.

Mamie decided that the next tune "Baby Please Don't Go" by Lightning Hopkins would play without her trademark narrative preceding it. Willie deserved as much.

"Where are you, Willie?"

Silence. Mamie stepped up her urgency. "Willie?"

"I'm right here. Right where it all happened. Right where my beloved left me and where I'll leave this world and see her in the next."

"You're at the accident site? Are you in your car?"

"That's right, Mamie. You can call the cops if you think it will help. But it won't. It's already done."

"What's already done? Willie, nothing is done. You don't have to go this way."

"I already have, Mamie. So how about you grant a dying man his last request and play the song."

"Willie, what the hell are you talking about? What's already done?"

"You were right about me, Mamie." Willie's voice was slow and heavy, minutes away from slumber. "I could never take my own life with a gun."

"You could never take your own life, Willie. Now sit tight and let me come to you."

"Oh, that's sweet, Mamie. I do appreciate your concern, but you'll never make it in time."

"Why not?"

Silence.

"Why not, Willie?"

"Because I already swallowed a handful of pills. Been washing them down with a steady flow of whiskey since your show began." His voice was slow and starting to slur. Mamie's neck grew cold and her stomach dropped as she was overcome with the same helpless feeling as when she first heard about her family.

"Willie. Wait there. I'll be right there."

"You'll never make it, Mamie. You'll just find another dead soul at a crossroads that's already hosted enough departure."

"God damn you, Willie!"

"Maybe you're right. I'll be gone soon. Maybe damned to Hell. It's not in my hands. But I'm done with this world and could really use some exit music."

Mamie held her silence for as long as she could bear until the tears filled her eyes and rolled from her cheeks to the grime of the ashtray below.

"This isn't fair, Willie."

"None of it is, but I'm still sorry." His voice was slow; the rpm of his vocal chords had been set to the wrong speed. He didn't have long.

She put the line on hold, bent to her crate of records and pulled out her copy of "Let Me Hold You." She remembered the day her friend and blues mentor, "Sweet" Sam Berry, first played her the record. To Mamie, listening to the song that first time was like being born. Every listen since then had been like going home.

Though she wasn't a legal relation, Mamie was Sam's only family and would learn this truth the day Sam died with only she at his bedside.

Before passing on, he bequeathed to Mamie his entire record collection, a lifetime of crate digging and a trove of blues that would become the foundation for the Midnight Blues radio show.

Sam had a request before he moved on. He had no illusions about the crossroads at which he'd arrived, but before he ventured to the other side he wanted to hear Audrey Jackson sing "Let Me Hold You" one last time.

That was eleven years ago. The record was a collectible *then*. Lord knows what it was worth today. If Mamie ever bothered to spend more than two minutes online she could probably find out, but she never did. Her blues weren't for sale.

Sam had closed his eyes sometime during the second and final guitar solo, never to open them again. Mamie pictured his face as it looked when his soul left this world, listening to the song Willie had requested to hear before ending his own life. She thought of her husband and son, wondering if they too had been listening to the same song when their car collided with Willie's.

This record. This flat, seven-inch sphere of polyvinyl chloride with a peeling label had been the ominous link to the death of so many for whom Mamie cared. Now it was poised to take another.

For a moment, she considered smashing the record over the console, an impulsive move of destruction that would render it impossible for her to acquiesce to a suicidal caller's last request. Then she caught a glimpse of her family. She locked onto their enduring image long enough to gather herself.

Lightnin' Hopkins brought "Baby Please Don't Go" to a close and Mamie leaned into the mic.

"We've reached the end of our show for tonight. I'll leave you with this story about love and redemption."

Mamie lit a smoke, took a drag, and exhaled a romantic haze of diffusion into the studio. The mood was set for the signature moment of the Midnight Blues radio show.

"Pour yourself a drink, light one up, sit back, and let me tell you a story."

Mamie glanced at her family. There was no way to know for sure how many people might be listening to her on the air tonight, but she knew there was one.

Willie was out there. He was waiting at the crossroads, a toxic cocktail of booze and pills taking his bloodstream hostage. He'd made his choice, and there was nothing Mamie could do about it. She closed her eyes and told her audience the story it wanted to hear.

"It was 1971. Nixon was in the White House, *All in the Family* made its small screen debut, and cigarette advertising was banned from radio and television.

"Audrey Jackson didn't know a thing about politics or television. She was an unknown Gospel singer from Statesboro, Georgia who was as poor as a wandering field hand but had a set a pipes that could make the devil weep. She'd come to Florida's Ybor City during a July whose swelter made the resident black folks long for a South Carolina plantation.

"No one knows for sure when she met Johnny Colton, but according to legend, it was love at first song on a Friday night on Ybor's famed Seventh Avenue.

"Johnny and Audrey were a star-crossed pair from the start. He was a poor street performer with a Fender strat across his back and a Pignose amp at his side. She was a passerby looking for work who was seduced by the lure of an ax man making every note bend to his will.

"Audrey jumped into one of his sidewalk jams and almost made Johnny flub a note when he heard her sing. It was like God had personally blessed her voice with the burden of man. You could hear the power and emotion from two blocks away. Listeners flocked to Seventh Avenue just be closer to the source and get a glimpse of the earth angel who was belting out the ragged perfection.

"Johnny and Audrey improvised twelve bar standards on that very corner to the delight of hundreds, and by midnight had earned enough money for a bottle of whiskey, a night at the Don Vicente hotel, and three hours of recording time, which Johnny promptly booked with Sleazy Sid Chambers at Chamber studios.

"Sid, Johnny knew from experience, was a stickler for time and would've kicked John Lennon out of his studio if he didn't pay for his session up front. Fortunately for Johnny and Audrey, the only thing Sid liked more than clean books was a good single malt—a weakness that played into Johnny's strength when he won a bottle of the best whiskey in Ybor after besting the namesake owner of Charlie Ray's pool hall in a game of nine ball. The winnings would be enough to get Sid passed out or render him unconcerned with the time overage it would take to properly record 'Let me Hold You.'

"Sleazy Sid may have been sauced by two o'clock that day, but not from Johnny's bottle. Johnny and Audrey recorded "Let Me Hold You" in a single take. They paid the scrupulous studio owner in cash and gave him the bottle of single malt as a gesture in good faith.

"No one knows for sure who the other cats who played on the record were. Dozens of limelight searchers have since claimed they were in the studio that day, but nothing's ever been proven. Like so much of the early blues, the identity of the supporting cast is shrouded in fabled mystique. Legendary blues sessions don't often involve a roll sheet.

"Apparently Sleazy Sid found something more in the work of Johnny and Audrey than a mere day's pay. When the police finally found him, his massive body was sprawled on the floor of his control room. Heart failure was ruled the official cause of death.

"As the story goes, 'Let Me Hold You' was in the take-up position on the console's main reel, having been the last song Sleazy Sid would ever playback before his soul stepped from the face of the Earth. He had the bottle Johnny had gifted him in his hand and a smile on his face. The crusty man went happy, so the legend goes.

"Johnny knew the recording of 'Let Me Hold You' was the couple's future, a calling card to fortune. He had the dream planned in full. Once the world heard the seraphic sounds of his lover's vocals it would melt just as he had. He may have been right, but the world never got the chance. Nothing comes easy with the blues, dreams included.

"Johnny and Audrey never made it to Atlanta and Sire Records where the dream was supposed to begin with the recording of the full-length LP that would feature 'Let Me Hold You' as its first single. Just after crossing the border and heading north into Georgia, the duo was stopped by Jessup county's sheriff department. Johnny was issued a ticket for driving with an inoperable headlight. That much is official and a matter of record. The true punishment was much more severe than the crime. Local members of the Ku Klux Klan didn't take too kindly to a white man driving a black woman through their zip code.

"The bodies turned up about a mile into the woods off of Highway 75. Johnny had been bludgeoned to death. Audrey was repeatedly raped before she met the same fate as her lover. The usual investigation ensued. A formality and an exercise in paperwork. Nothing more. This was the South in the early 1970's. A backward land whose climate would never fully adjust to society's racial edicts, no matter how often they were televised.

"Johnny Colton and Audrey Jackson were victims soon forgotten by a world denied of their talents. Sire records would release 'Let Me Hold You' in 1972 on a limited pressing of a thousand units to little fanfare and paltry sales. The label went belly up later in the year. Then came the fire at the label's warehouse, which would naturally be suspected of arson and duly investigated. Nothing would ever be proven, but the insurance claims would more than compensate for the lost inventory, which included several hundred copies of 'Let Me Hold You'.

Mamie took another pull from her flask.

"This is the last song of the show, and it goes out to all of you who have lost, but still press on. That's what…" her voice trailed off as she broke her gaze on her family by closing her eyes. She took a deep breath and wondered if Willie was still listening or if he too had moved on. Mamie decided it didn't matter one way or the other.

"That's what the blues is really about. Surviving. Enduring. So if you're out there hurting, but you still believe and you're still fighting…this song's for you. I'm Mamie Rogers. You've been listening to Midnight Blues on WMLN. With Johnny Colton on the lead guitar, this is Audrey Jackson with 'Let Me Hold You.'"

She dropped the needle on the record, took a swig from her flask, and clicked back to the phone line. "So long, Willie. Tell the devil I'll see him when I do."

She dumped the call, lit a cigarette, and listened to "Let Me Hold You." The song opened with a fade in, a rare motif then as it is now. The slow ramp up in volume sounded like the song had been playing for some time, and only now was the listener aware of it and allowed to peer into the performer's soul.

This was blues that took its time. Slow blues, played by cats who knew how to lay back and let their fellow player emote. Johnny's guitar and Audrey's voice sounded like tormented lovers kept apart by circumstance, hopeful that they'll one day soon reunite, contented to press on until they do.

Baby come on over here. Let me hold you...

Mamie thought of what Audrey Jackson must have felt in the minutes before her end. The gospel singer from Statesboro had a lifetime of love and heartbreak in front of her until her future was stolen by racist hands.

...In my arms. Let me hold you in my arms.

She thought about what might be going through Willie's mind as he listened to the diva's vibrato, letting it seep into what remained of his soul here on Earth.

I want to be...I want to be...your lover.

There was nothing she could do for him. Willie had made his choice. As she took another swig from her flask, she reminded herself that a man with a death wish can't be saved. Not by God. Not by the blues.

Mamie listened to 'Let Me Hold You' for another verse. Then she reached across the console, past her family's picture, grabbed her car keys, and headed for the door.

Larissa's Friday Night Earthquake

Larissa was in the perfect mind for a weekend of agoraphobia. The prospect of spending her Friday night binging on a marathon of *Ace of Cakes* on the Food Network had promise. Maybe she'd down a bottle of pinot grigio or, better yet, swallow a fistful of pills and see how much ice cream she could kill before she passed out.

She'd rather be anywhere than out in the world and around people. Carlo was a person, and he was somewhere in the world, which meant she was safer in her apartment where the pinot, valium, and Cherry Garcia were in long supply.

Her phone vibrated against the coffee table. If it was her mom, she would toss the thing in the fish tank. She'd rather sit in the third circle of hell playing Go-Fish with every ex-boyfriend she'd ever had than listen to another lecture from her mom about biological clocks and women approaching forty.

It was Kelly. She wasn't calling for a lecture. She was calling to lift her friend out of a funk by taking her out into the world with the girls. Jesus, they were a pathetic lot, weren't they? Each was closer to 40 than 30, going out for a Friday night on the town as if life's answers could be found in the bottom of a fruity shot that came in a test tube served by some twenty-two-year-old with a rack that could steal a reality show.

Pathetic, Larissa thought.

Two weeks ago she wasn't pathetic. Two weeks ago she had Carlo. They were out on a Friday night at the kind of bar you felt superior in when you had your arm around your man. The house looked at you with envy, and you beamed because deep down you knew the skinny girls had tried every trick in Cosmo to hone their looks and charm so they could catch a man like the one you had. The skanks with the comic book racks wore heels that were higher and tops that were tighter because they wanted what you *had*.

Had was the operative word. She had a boyfriend, with potential. She had the kind of whimsical security that makes you pity single girls when you spot one alone on a Friday night and shame them when they're in groups. She had an identity. She had a life.

Now she was the single one, and Kelly wanted to take her out to mingle among the desperately-seeking as though Larissa were a convicted prison guard forced to live in general population as an inmate. Kelly had all the friend-of-the-broken-hearted cliches locked and loaded.

You have to get back out there.

The best way to get over the last one is with the next one.

I know it's scary, but time heals a broken—

"Fuck that," Larissa thought. There's never been a trite line that Tori Amos couldn't make better. Maybe that was how she'd spend tomorrow night, listening to *Little Earthquakes*...again, only this time with a mound of buttered popcorn and a bottle of vodka. Not a bad idea, if she lived through tonight.

The phone stopped vibrating, and Larissa relaxed like a torture victim between electric shocks. She should get up, get moving, if only around the apartment. Maybe she could dance, work up some endorphins if she had any left in her decaying thirty-seven-year-old body. Just getting up seemed pointless. It all seemed pointless.

She wasn't startled when Kelly poked her head through the window and was even a bit impressed when she pulled her size 14 body through the open frame with the ease of a gymnast sticking a tough landing.

Kelly plopped down on the couch and strapped her heels to her feet. "Wouldn't be much of a rescue if I died on the fire escape, so I had to go barefoot."

"How'd you make it the first twenty feet?" Larissa asked. It was a legitimate question now that she was single and freshly concerned about strangers being able to ascend from street level to the fire escape above and infiltrate her apartment.

"There's a crew of painters down there," Kelly with wry sarcasm. "I showed 'em my boobs and they let me use their extension ladder."

Larissa knew there was about an 80% chance she was telling the truth. Kelly's boobs had been refined tools of manipulation since the eighth grade. Flashing was a strategy she had regularly employed in her twenties, when she and her body had the upper hand against gravity. Larissa almost smiled when she recalled the time they were eleven bucks short of cab fare after a night of boozing in Ybor City until dawn. Kelly settled the bill with one mighty pull off her top that unleashed her girls on a cabbie who hailed from a place where women aren't allowed to bare the skin of their ankles. He never stood a chance.

Larissa spent the next year reminding Kelly that her boobs had a street value of $5.50 a piece. Kelly was always quick to defend that they were worth more in offices.

"Ok!" Kelly clapped her hands like a camp counselor hellbent on making the next activity sound more fun than it really was. "Let's get you hot and fabulous."

"I'm not going out."

"Don't make me force-funnel three Red Bulls down your throat."

Larissa silently chastised herself for thinking Kelly would attack with anything but originality.

"I was thinking about smoking a joint and vegging," she replied with about as much energy as a hungover teen.

Kelly shook her head. "Weed is for weekdays. Besides, we did that twice this week, and now it's Friday night. So, up and in the shower. I'll start the hot water and pick out your outfit."

"Ugggghhhh," was all Larissa could manage. Kelly took her exasperation as a sign of progress.

Larissa's coffee table was festooned with the junk of a depressed shut-in, yet Kelly managed to extract the CD case to *Little Earthquakes* from beneath a mound of vapid knick-knacks like she knew it was there all along. The seminal album by Tori Amos had been an anthem for the pair since they first discovered it in middle school. Each track spun lyrics that cut right to the heart of the female soul. The two friends would listen to the album together from end to end at regular intervals in the 20 years since, when one or both of them had been beaten down by parents, by boys, or just by life.

It was one of the last CD's Larissa still owned. Kelly held it in her hands and studied the relic's back cover art way a good Christian looks at the Sistine Chapel. The illustration of two growing mushrooms had taken on different meanings over the years, but from day one they looked like penises. One tall and skinny, the other short and fat. Each spoke different truths about life and a woman's struggle, depending on how either felt about men at the particular time. Sometimes you were the tall one, able to rise above it all. The rest of the time your were squat from being beaten down and deprived of oxygen. Either way you were left in a world of dicks.

The album had been on repeat for the last three days, providing a soundtrack Larissa hoped would keep her from drowning in a pool of guilt and self-loathing. It wasn't working.

Kelly tossed the case, penis side up, on the coffee table and said, "Tori can only do so much. I'm here to take you the rest of the way."

Larissa rolled her eyes. "Where're we going?"

Kelly shot her friend a knowing smirk and said, "Dancing."

* * * * *

Larissa felt like every finger in the room was pointing at her as soon as she and Kelly entered the club. Everyone in the place looked like they had come straight from an Abercrombie and Fitch cover shoot. They all had air-brushed skin and bodies that would make a Greek goddess renew her gym membership. Larissa felt like a flea-bag mutt at the Westminster Kennel show.

The music made her feel old and tired. It was too loud, too fast, too unrecognizable. There was an app for that, right? One that told you what song was playing? Wouldn't do any good, Larissa thought. She needed a time machine to take her back to when she wasn't so pitiful. And if it couldn't go that far back, she'd settle for when she had Carlo.

Kelly grabbed Larissa's hand and led the pair into the fray. She had a plan. Kelly always had a plan. There wasn't a twenty-something waif on the planet who could rattle her confidence. Maybe one day, Larissa thought, she'll be her own, like Kelly, but not tonight.

Larissa squeezed her friend's hand, fearing what might happen if she let go and had to swim on her own in the sea of beautiful people. Drowning in a pool of depression was one thing, but sinking to the ocean floor past the reefs of chiseled torsos and size twos was a humiliation she couldn't bear.

They docked at the bar and Larissa found herself anchored next to a guy with the body of a pro athlete. Tall, cut, and cocksure the way guys in $1000 jeans tend to be. She didn't give a shit about sports and never cared one way or another about the jocks who played them, but maybe that's because she never went for one. She searched her mind for the names of the players Carlo knew so well from years devoted to fantasy football, or maybe it was baseball. She cursed herself for not having paid attention to the details when they were together.

The guy shifted his frame and revealed a pair of girls who hung on his every word and whatever else he would offer later that night. Both looked like they could stand in for Angelina Jolie—not the mother of six (or however many kids Angie was up to these days) but the *Gone in Sixty Seconds* starlet who could steal any man with nothing more than a lustful stare. It was just as well she didn't have a clever intro line. The guy was out of her league, no matter what the sport was.

Kelly thrust two drinks at Larissa. One was a clear shot, the other the kind of colorful concoction that, in this place, probably costs more than the minimum wage. She knew better than to question what she was about to consume and raised her shot glass to meet Kelly's.

Larissa yelled over the music, "What are we drinking to?"

"To fucking freedom," Kelly shouted, then threw back her shot like its contents might otherwise evaporate. Larissa followed suit. Vodka. It met her tongue like a VIP and slid down her throat with a grace reserved for top shelf spirits.

"Where are the girls?" Larissa asked as she plopped her empty shot glass on the bar with a force someone from across the room might actually mistake for confidence.

"They're home, icing their vaginas," Kelly said with an air that let Larissa know diminished numbers weren't going to squash their adventure. Larissa felt relieved. She didn't want attention. She wanted to evaporate and the vodka helped.

Kelly handed her another shot.

Larissa took it and committed herself to getting so drunk she wouldn't care if she slept in her makeup.

She said wryly, "To fucking freedom?"

"How about single and successful?"

Larissa swallowed her shot and felt compelled to take stock of her professional life. She'd worked harder in her 20's than any of these club rats would ever know, earned every promotion like a soldier earns her medals of valor. If corporate America awarded Purple Hearts, Larissa would have at least three. One for the time Larry Meltzer spilled coffee on her white blouse two minutes before she had to present the yearly projections to the board of directors, another for the time she had to pose for a picture while sitting on the lap of an over-served Jeffery Mancuso at the company Christmas party, and a third just for putting up with alpha-dominated sales team that wouldn't know the meaning of harassment if they were forced to share a jail cell in a French prison with Harvey Weinstein.

The brain that had earned her straight A's since birth, had taken her to the doldrums of middle management as an adult. She made financial reports that helped the brass keep accurate score. At least she could fire people, but she hadn't. Instead, she'd spent countless after-hours writing letters of recommendation to help her flock get their promotions and their bonuses. Not that her altruism merited reciprocation. Her career had flattened and was resting in a place where skepticism seemed the perfect tonic for jealousy and laziness.

Maybe her brain had taken her as far as she was meant to go. Didn't some guy coin a principle for hitting your intellect's professional ceiling? She should Google it. Whipping out her iPhone would make her look like she fit into this place. Or she could just drink. Her tired brain wouldn't mind being robbed of a few cells by way of alcohol. It could use the night off.

She hadn't planned on working forever. There was a logical path she was going to follow that wasn't all that different from the one most girls decide on when they realize *Cinderella* is only a myth. Her plan involved things she would *get*. She would *get* married. She would *get* pregnant. She would *get* to quit her job so she could raise her children in a world that didn't involve adultery and quarterly reports. That life is a fairy tale. Some girls get to live in it, but not her. To commiserate that truth, she was going to *get* drunk.

The chill had worn off in the club. The vodka had clocked in and Larissa was entering the place where she saw herself in the world around her.

She spotted a girl on the dance floor who looked like a *Devil's Advocate*-era Charlize Theron, confident the way she would be if she were that tall and beautiful and sure she could take home any guy she wanted, or no one if she wasn't in the mood and just wanted to dance.

Larissa reached from her perch at the bar and tapped the goddess on the shoulder.

Excuse me, but can I be you for a while? I need a break from myself, and you seemed like as good an escape as any. I could tell you the details, But I don't want to bore. I just want to own this place for a while and I thought being you could help. No, no, just your body. I'll keep my own brain. Love the shoes. Christian Louboutin, right? I can tell by the red soles. By the way, where do I let him…shoot? Just kidding, if the guy doesn't have his own condoms I should send him home…right?

Larissa snapped back to herself. Had she really just taken another shot? She could feel the ice around her inhibitions liquifying. Boys get discovered when vodka melts the winter. She saw one on the dance floor and could tell he was holding back. Larissa could see he had more than he was showing because the supermodel he was with had two left feet. It happens that way, doesn't it? Girls with looks find themselves paired with guys they don't deserve. This guy could dance.

Larissa didn't know the song that was blasting from the house's system at a decibel level she could feel between her toes. It was soulless dreck, made palatable through the wonders of pitch-correction software. But there was a groove. It found her the way rhythm had since she heard her first Janet Jackson song when she was eight.

She had taken to dancing the way closet drinkers befriend alcohol. It started in middle school, something she did on weekends with friends. She had realized early that not only did it make her feel good, but she was good at it so she did it more when no one was looking. She found dancing to be a tonic for teenage depression, collegiate stress, post-graduate tension, and lower middle-age anxiety. Lock the front door. Clear the living room. Crank the music to an obnoxious level, and dance like no one is watching—leave it all on the floor and sweat so hard you have to take a cold shower after.

Larissa couldn't tell that her hips were in lockstep with the meter of the song, but anyone observing the bar would have seen a tier of twenty-somethings lost in small talk and one thirty-seven year old locked into the groove. Her eyes were latched onto the dance floor and it wasn't until Kelly snatched her hand that she broke her trance.

"Let's dance," Kelly said, leading the way to the floor. Larissa heard Tori's lyric in her head *like Judy Garland taking a female Buddha by the hand.*

"Kelly, I'm not so—."

"Yes, you are."

Before Larissa could argue, Kelly had knifed a path to the club's epicenter and launched Larissa to the heart of the dance floor where a kaleidoscope of colored light rained from above. Tight bodies gyrated in all directions around her, but they slipped out of focus. The music took on a new life as if the club's sound system was calibrated to project every ounce of its fidelity on the exact spot where Larissa was standing. The beat that rattled her toes while she had stood at the bar now timed with her own heartbeat on the dance floor.

She felt naked. Look, she thought, I'm standing naked before you. But no one was looking, except for Kelly who was dancing a beat behind the song but had otherwise assimilated with the vibe of the crowd. Her best friend since the sixth grade was the original circus girl without a safety net, completely unconcerned with the paralyzing details of self-awareness. She had succeeded in springing Larissa from a self-imposed sentence of domestic self-loathing. Now here they were, the oldest pair on the dance floor, each with at least $50 of top-shelf booze in them.

She could feel the beat in her chest. The music that was unrecognizable a moment ago suddenly became familiar. The DJ had cued a throwback hit that galvanized the crowd. Janet

Jackson's "Rhythm Nation" engulfed the club and Larissa half expected the diva herself to hit the floor through a cloud of stage smoke and a spate of strobe lights.

Janet Jackson didn't walk onto the dance floor that night, but Charlize Theron did— her doppelgänger at least. The statuesque blonde Larissa had observed from the bar strutted into the fray, which immediately parted and formed a circle around its goddess. Charlize was used to the attention and gave the crowd what it came to see. She executed a rapid-fire routine of moves that were worthy of MTV, though the millennials in the place would have recognized them from watching music videos on YouTube.

Charlize was good, and maybe it was the vodka's suggestion but Larissa knew she was better. She spun her head to check her surroundings. All eyes were on the Charlize. She was safe among the onlookers, content to watch someone else be glorified for what she believed in her introverted heart she could do better.

Larissa felt a hand take position above her waist. She cocked her head and met Kelly's eyes. With a hearty shove, Larissa was jettisoned from the crowd to the spotlight, where she bumped into Charlize, who shot her an immediate look of disgust that said *this is my scene. It was written for me. You're an extra, at best.*

Larissa would have played the part of the background dancer on most nights, but on this one, she was in the mood to try out for the starring role. She knew every move from the "Rhythm Nation" video, having seen the black and white masterpiece a thousand times during its initial run on MTV. The moves were second nature to her. Only the live audience and their ogling eyes could keep Larissa from showing her stuff. The vodka had done its part in eating away her shyness. Now it was her turn. She danced like she was alone in her apartment. She moved and the crowd responded with a swell of cheer.

Charlize responded, too. She may have been 10 years younger than Larissa, but she too had studied Miss Jackson's nasty moves and showed off a few to let the crowd know who was the reigning queen of the club's dance floor. Larissa thought about returning to the safety of the sidelines. She'd made her point. Hadn't she? She picked out a spot for her retreat, only to find a familiar face. Carlo. He wasn't alone. He was with a girl. *Girl* was the right word. Even through her vodka-goggles, Larissa could see Carlo's new squeeze was barely old enough to be in this place.

She turned away just as Charlize finished her move to the delight of the crowd, then held her pose and stared Larissa down as if to dare her to top what she'd just pulled off.

A few cheers from the house urged Larissa to answer the challenge. The Friday night crowd wanted a show, or maybe they just wanted to see Larissa embarrass herself. She couldn't bear to look back at Carlo, so she picked up the routine where Charlize had left off. Her hips popped. Her legs snapped. The audience reacted to all of it. Charlize watched like an itchy-fingered guitarist waiting for her chance to solo.

Larissa added a few steps of her own creativity to the routine and threw the spotlight back to Charlize with a detectable air of defiance that the crowd loved. Charlize returned the favor with a mocking nod of her own. She stepped up her moves in a way Larissa could see were playing to the blonde's physical gifts. The lunges went deeper, her long legs kicked higher. Maybe she'd been a gymnast. Maybe she was an NFL cheerleader.

By now, Larissa knew what she'd gotten herself into. This was a dance-off. An old-school battle of moves and skill, with no defined prize, save for bragging rights and respect. Sides had been drawn amongst the audience. Charlize was dancing to win. Larissa was quickly realizing she had nothing to lose.

Charlize was more than a body. She was a dancer. Her moves had the kind of class that comes with professional grooming. For a moment, Larissa forgot she was in a battle and watched Charlize like the rest of the fans in the club. The flashing lights grabbed her curves in all the right places. Even the sweat she'd worked up looked sexy. Larissa doubted that the sweat she'd broken out in looked as hot. Was this a hot flash? Jesus, she wasn't that old. The bouncers at places like this check for menopause, don't they?

Charlize threw it back to Larissa with a club-ready pirouette that ended in perfect cool. Larissa expected this one to win the crowd for good. She could retire to the bar with her head held high. A few might even pat her on the back and buy her a shot for having the guts to take on a supermodel in a dance off, herself a mere plus-sized mortal.

Larissa peeked back at the spot where Carlo had been. He was still there, watching. She'd never danced in front of him before, never had the courage to let go. *This is a piece of me you've never seen.* Maybe he liked the show. Maybe he'd urge her to answer the bell and give everything she had for one final round. Maybe she'd win and he'd realize he'd been wrong, that she was the one all along.

Fuck Cinderella, Larissa thought. No one needs an invitation to the ball. She turned her head back to the floor and never saw Carlo's reaction, whatever it may have been. She wanted to dance.

The song had reached its breakdown, the percussive section where the best dancers in the video showed their best stuff. In the video, the dancers had multiple takes at their disposal to get it right and wow the audience. Larissa knew she had one.

The crowd had grown and it appeared everyone in the club was watching the dance floor and the one-on-one battle that had arrived at its climax. Charlize stared Larissa down with a glare that aimed to finish her opponent off. There was a hint of respect in her eyes, the way the favorite allows the underdog a consolatory sense of satisfaction.

Even though it was Larissa's turn, Charlize launched into her routine. It was obvious to Larissa and anyone watching that this stanza of the performance was meant to be a knockout blow. Larissa held on to the groove as she watched Charlize pull off an impossibly high kick of her leg, followed by a split that defied physics. The crowd gasped when her torso dropped to the floor. They cheered when she popped back to her feet like a martial artist poised to continue the fight. She had perfect balance, a dancer's grace, and a showman's flair for the dramatic. If Janet Jackson had walked into the club at that moment, she would have offered this girl a contract and a one-way ticket on a time machine headed for 1989.

Charlize's final maneuver was unlike anything she'd unleashed thus far in the contest. Her moves were flawless, just as her previous had been, just like everything about her seemed to be. This time she brought her routine to a dazzling finish by turning her back to Larissa, then reaching her hand to the sky in exact time with the music's culminating beat. The crowd roared. She held the pose for a diva's moment, then looked back at Larissa with her trademark stare. She added a wink as if to thank Larissa for playing. Then she walked off the floor. The crowd parted for her as she advanced through it, and closed behind her as if to encircle the queen in the populace's love. It was the dance-off equivalent of a mic drop. Larissa knew she didn't have a chance.

Charlize's routine had lasted the whole of the song's breakdown. An observant DJ would have looped the track so Larissa would get her fair shake. Instead, the song played on and Larissa rolled with it, figuring this wasn't the kind of place where you could file a protest.

She hit the first beat one cue and stepped into a litany of b-boy moves that were a throwback to the 1980s. She started with the Chinese Typewriter, jumping side to side while reversing her toes in and out a la MC Hammer. Next, she backed the bus up, hands on an imaginary steering wheel, she leaned her ass to the center of the dance floor and walked backward checking both mirrors while cramping the wheel. The audience roared. Larissa gave some more gas.

Next came the Hello Kitty—feet together, she opened her legs by spreading her knees then closed them as she slowly descended. Just as she hit the bottom floor, Larissa pushed off her knees while arching her back and sticking her ass out on an express trip back to a fully upright position. This one brought another cheer from the gallery. It also brought Charlize back to the floor to check on the competition.

Larissa went straight into the Ed Lover. With both arms to the side, she stepped directly at Charlize with her right foot and simultaneously popped her right hip. She did the same with the left, then the right, all the while locking her eyes on Charlize and closing the space between them until the two were within intimate distance. Larissa held the gaze for a beat, then moonwalked a few feet to create some space for the finale.

There were only a few measures the song left. Larissa's final move needed to bring the house down. A breakdancing windmill was in order. She dropped her right hand to the floor then dropped the rest of her body to give the momentum needed to spin her upper chest, shoulders, and back in tight circles on the floor while twirling her legs through the air in a V-shape. As her momentum slowed, she regained speed by pulling her knees to her chest. She held the spinning top position for the last few beats of the song, then thrust out her legs and propped her head on her hand just as the song ended. She finished the move in a classic lounge position, facing Charlize.

The crowd lost its mind. Larissa gave her opponent a sexy wink.

It's kind of funny the things you think of at times like these. As the crowd rushed the dance floor, Larissa felt like she was in a little earthquake of her own. *Am I about to be trampled? I'm not complaining. At least I'll go out on a cool note.* She closed her eyes to enjoy the moment, even if it were destined to include a death by stampede. She imagined the headlines on Facebook as news of her freakish passing spread amongst her friends. "Girl wins dance-off, killed by the crowd that loved her." Had she really won?

A pair of arms reached around her torso and pulled her to her feet. She wondered what she would do if it were Carlo. Would she open her eyes and kiss him passionately on the mouth, forgiving everything in a single gesture of love and faith? Or would she punch him square in the face and knock him out right here on the dance floor? Maybe she'd kick him in the balls before he staggered to the fetal position.

Larissa opened her eyes and found Kelly, who said something mostly inaudible save for the word "badass." She hugged her best friend, who'd saved her from a night self-loathing and junk food, who'd gotten her on her feet when all she wanted to do was melt into the scenery of life's periphery, where she could drift without fear of being judged or hurt.

Charlize pushed her way through the crowd to Larissa. The two locked eyes and Larissa saw that she really was beautiful in a way most people aren't. Her looks ensured that she would never sneak up on anyone for the rest of her life, but right now she wasn't interested in standing out. She leaned into Larissa's ear and said, "Can you teach me that move?"

Larissa grinned and answered, "Breakdance training starts at the bar in five minutes." Charlize nodded with a smile like a kid who had something to look forward to. Kelly planted a giant smooch on Larissa's cheek like she used to do in the high school halls on a weekly basis. All around them, the crowd Larissa had won over danced and rejoiced like this was their last Friday night on Earth.

Larissa scanned the crowd for Carlo, just to see if the look on his face might reveal what he was thinking in this, her moment of redemptive glory. She found the boy who could dance and who now seemed less interested in the rhythmically challenged waif at his side. Their eyes met and he sent Larissa the kind of smile that invites an impish future.

Carlo was nowhere in sight.

Buy Here, Pay Here

The first one to speak loses. That's what O.C. says. You sit there in absolute silence, for as long as it takes, until the customer breaks. Then you kill him.

O.C. loved to talk about the time he held his tongue for two hours while this cowboy from Texarkana stared at the paperwork for a 1982 Silverado with a two and a half inch lift. Two hours. Not a damn sound, except the for second hand on the clock on the wall. When O.C. tells the story, that second-hand gets so loud it sounds like a pendulum with a sickle attached to its end. Who's it going to slice in half? The guy who speaks first, that's who. First one to open his yap loses. That's what O.C. says.

Jessie hadn't said a word for about a minute. A few months ago, the one minute mark was about when he'd start to feel the puddles under his arms. He was tougher now, confident the customer would always break first.

The deal was for a '98 Taurus with a sticker price of thirty-five hundred, but the kill was in the financing. Guy walks onto the lot, he's an *up*. That's what O.C. says. An up isn't a customer until you engage him and figure out if he's just a tire kicker looking to waste everyone's time.

We don't have tire kickers here, O.C. says. Up walks onto the lot, he wants to buy. Up walks onto the lot where the sign says *buy here, pay here*, he wants to be killed.

They can't get no love anyplace else, O.C.says. They got no credit, so the banks won't touch 'em. If the banks won't touch 'em, the big shiny dealerships are gonna treat 'em like they got the plague. They're screwed anywhere they go, except here. So we love 'em, O.C. says. Treat 'em like they belong, like nothing's their fault. Hell, it ain't their fault, O.C. says. Is it a man's fault he falls on hard times? Is it his fault the world's gone to shit and I'm sorry fella, I know you've got kids, but we got to lay you off? Hell if it is, O.C. says. A man finds hard times in this life as sure as the Tampa sun rises in the on the land-side of the beach, but he still needs a ride. He still needs financing.

You're OK to ride! reads the sign on the chain-link fence with a barbed wire top that bounds O.C.'s lot. Other places in town try to be cute with their signs. They say things like *No Credit? Forget it!* or *If you got a job…you ride.* Makes a man who's down feel inferior, O.C. says. An up feels inferior, he's got his guard up and if he's got his guard up, he's damn sure got one hand on his wallet because he thinks you're after him.

An up should never feel desperate, O.C. says. He needs to feel loved. When an up feels loved, he relaxes and drops his guard. When he drops his guard, he's yours for the kill.

Jessie settled his eyes on the customer sitting across the metal desk. The guy's brow furrowed as he stared at the deal like he was trying to calculate odds at a blackjack table, the first he'd ever sat at in his life. A customer with no game for negotiation is a *bunny.* That's what O.C. says. Jessie had this bunny locked in the kill zone.

The guy had been the first up on the lot that morning. He'd hopped off the bus at the stop on the corner of Broad Street and Nebraska Avenue. O.C. always preached to Jessie to be religious about watching the bus stop, because an up who takes the bus to a car lot is looking to buy a lot more than a car. He's looking for dignity, but he'll pay extra for respect.

O.C. had made sure that the window in the single-wide on the lot that doubled as the sales office had a clear view of the bus stop. Jessie had seen the Saturday morning crowd descend from the bus and scatter in the usual directions. A typical portion went straight for the Alpine Liquor Store on the Northwest corner of the block. A handful crossed the street on their way to the E-Z Pawn shop, whose marquis reminded to *lay-a-way for X-Mas day* even though it was July. A lone rider broke from the pack and turned south toward O.C.'s.

Jessie had watched him from the window. O.C. was at his side like a football coach watching the opponent's pre-game warm-ups with his quarterback, imparting a few last minute adjustments to the game plan before the battle began.

"Brother's gonna have to wash that shirt if he wants to wear it again for church tomorrow," O.C. said as the up turned into the lot. The morning sun bombed the man's white Oxford and reflected a white glare. The guy didn't have a jacket, not because it was already almost 90 degrees, O.C. pointed out. He looked like a Bible salesman struggling to make his monthly quota, the kind who'd go without a jacket even in winter if it meant saving a few green backs.

"I'm not making a joke, son," O.C. said. "Guy's trying to look respectable. Probably wearing the best shirt he owns. So you make sure you compliment him on it when you introduce yourself. Make him feel loved."

The up made his way onto the lot and went straight to line of sedans parked against the fence. "Look here, son," O.C. said. "I got three cars in that row that this man's eyeing. He wants that Dodge, but at fifty-five hundred he knows he can't afford it. He can afford that Mitsubishi at nineteen."

"So I sell him that one?" Jessie asked.

"Please, son. Black man has no business in a rice-burner. Especially if it's used. You're gonna show him the Dodge and let him see what he can't have. Then you're gonna show him the rice cooker and let him see what he can afford, but don't want. Then you're gonna sell him the Taurus, which is gonna look like a deal from God at thirty-five."

His name was Josiah. That's what he'd said when Jessie asked right after complimenting him on his shirt. Jessie had employed the F.O.R.D.S. system and bled the man of his basic story while the two test drove the Taurus down Nebraska Avenue and circled back up Florida Avenue.

O.C. says you can have a conversation with anyone if you stick with F.O.R.D.S. All you have to do is ask the right questions.

Family: the guy had 4 kids (three girls, one baby son)

Occupation: He was a reverend who worked odd jobs around Tampa when he could find them. He was starting a new job in Sulpher Springs and needed the car to get to and fro.

Recreation: He loved the Lord. He loved his family. He loved his church.

Dreams: He had no interest in being the man. He just wanted to provide.

School: Born and raised in Belmont Heights. Graduated from Hillsborough High.

Josiah was older than Jessie by about ten years if Jessie had to guess. Judging by the lines on his face and softness of his voice, they were the kind of hard years Jessie had no interest in experiencing for himself.

Josiah saw the world and everything in it as a blessing. Even the vagrants milling about Florida Avenue near the

Salvation Army were blessed. Jessie didn't buy it. The vagrants were looking for a handout and downright lucky there was a Salvation Army that would provide it. That, Josiah said, was the blessing.

Josiah held the wheel with his hands at ten and two like a student driver executing textbook form, a departure from the classic one-armed laid-back gangster pose most of the no-credit-cash-poor brothers strike as soon as they get behind the wheel for a test drive. He never came close to touching the radio and drove as though he were on the lookout for a ball to jump into the street followed by an unsuspecting kid.

They passed the big lots on Florida Avenue, each bustling with families of shoppers ogling the impressive rows of new and shiny Chevys, Fords, Toyotas and Nissans. Jessie saw them the way a shortstop in the bus leagues looked at Yankee stadium.

Back at the lot, he and Josiah sat in the parked Taurus. Jessie could tell Josiah liked the car by the way he still held onto the wheel even though the engine was idling. Josiah was visualizing, but Jessie could see he wasn't sure if he could afford the dream. That's when Jessie grabbed the keys from the ignition and uttered the most crucial line O.C. had taught him.

"Let's get out of this heat and run some numbers in my office," he said. It's never a question, O.C. says. You never give the customer an out by asking him if he *wants* to go back to your office. A salesman never asks. He suggests, then he gets out of the car and walks straight to the office and he doesn't look back.

He whistles if he has to like it's the most natural damn thing in the world to be getting out of the heat and into the air-conditioned negotiating pit. Oh, you'll want to look back, O.C. says, and see if the customer hasn't moved an inch, but you won't so much as glance over your shoulder until you reach the door and open it for him like he's royalty. Love him up. If he's following at your heels like a lost puppy, you know you got him.

Josiah had followed Jessie like a child in the wake of the Pied Piper. The outer appearance of the trailer was weather-beaten and didn't give much hope for the inside. That was O.C.'s plan. A customer walks into this office, O.C. says, he should be surprised and comfortable. This ain't your living room, son, with your laundry spilled on the couch and the pizza boxes piled on the coffee table. This here is a place of business. Man has to feel like this is where deals happen.

The office was clean but not impeccable, cool but not frigid, inviting but not overbearing. The walls had faux wood paneling adorned with framed pictures of Tampa, the kind they show snowbird tourists in brochures with skylines, cigar rollers, football players, and sunsets. O.C. had designed the place to be unassuming and natural, just like a good con man would.

Two minutes had passed, at least. Silence, save for the rumble of the wall-mounted air-conditioning unit, chugging and turning like a two-stroke engine in need of a new spark plug. Josiah hadn't budged. His eyes hadn't moved from the paperwork that lay on the desk in front of him.

The deal.

Somewhere in the next room, O.C. was standing by, ready to step in and close if Jessie felt weak in the stomach and needed his help. The only time it's a mistake to ask for help with the close is if it's after the customer has left the lot without buying, O.C. says. This here is a team game.

O.C. had drawn up the deal in his office, out of sight from Josiah. A salesmen's grin arched above his chin as he slid the paperwork to Jessie and eyed him like a proud father whose son has a deer locked in the crosshairs. The kill. It was Jessie's to make.

Josiah had a sob story. They've all got a sob story. Buyers are liars, O.C. says. That's them trying to sell you. The truth has nothing to do with the deal. Someone's always going through a divorce, or a job loss, or a mom who's old and sick. The only truth is that it's all part of the sell, O.C says. You listen. You nod your head. You say, "My Goodness!" And when they lay it on thick you say, "That's tragic!" Practice those two phrases until you've got as many ways to say them as the customer has excuses he can't buy, O.C. says. Keep saying them until the customer's story is all out of sob and there's nothing left but the deal, nothing left but the kill.

You're always trying to get to KFC, says O.C. Everybody wants to go to KFC! We're in the KFC business, O.C says

Kindness.

Financing.

Close.

Jessie's stomach clenched the way it did when he was knocking on the door of the close. He'd been working at O.C.'s for two months and had sold eight vehicles. The first was a 2002 Toyota Tercel with a hundred and twelve thousand miles on it to a nurse from Tampa Heights. She had eyes like Beyonce and a body like Queen Latifah. Her sob story was about her daughter with asthma and how the medical bills had wiped her clean and she needed the car to get to work so she could keep slaving to the man and earn a buck, and if there was any way Jessie could make the deal for 18.9% instead of 21 she'd do a dance and pray for him to be the most successful car salesmen in all of Tampa. What's 2.1%, Jessie had thought? Two little points and one-tenth of another on a loan for twenty-three-five. Even at 18.9, the deal was still a kill. Everybody wins, Jessie had thought, and so he'd taken the deal to O.C.

Jessie had written the numbers down and shown them to the customer. The second O.C. saw the chicken-scratched digits on the worksheet he leaned back in his chair and fixed Jessie with the stare of a disappointed father. Over the top of his cheaters, he locked his gaze onto Jessie and held his stare in silence. Jessie knew he'd failed.

"You wrote it down, kid," O.C. said. "It's an offer. Official as a welfare check. Now go back out there, tell her you can't believe the boss is gonna let the car ride at this rate, and she should sign before he comes to his senses."

Jessie backed toward the door, crestfallen, eyes downcast on the moldy carpet. "Kid," O.C. called, just before Jessie turned the knob. "Make sure you S.E.E."

<u>S</u>mile.

<u>E</u>ye contact.

<u>E</u>nthusiasm.

Salesmen loses his S.E.E. he loses his customer, O.C. says.

As soon as he opened the door, Jessie was sure this was his last day in the car business. He'd made the ultimate mistake and now he'd have to crawl back to Mr. James and beg for his old job on the lawn crew, sell him on how the car sales gig just wasn't for him and if there's any way he could be one of the weed trimmers again he'd never leave.

Sweat dripped down Jessie's back as he stood in the threshold between O.C.'s office and the sales desk. Had the paperwork in his hand spontaneously burst into flames, Jessie wouldn't have been surprised. He might have fallen on the flame, hoping he'd go up with it.

The deal was dead. The nurse was gone.

Jessie ran to windows, hoping to catch a glimpse of the woman. If he saw her, he could catch her and maybe even in turn her around.

"Damn lesson to be learned here, son," O.C. said, like an omniscient narrator to Jessie's flailing sales career. O.C. spoke directly. "Now, do I have to tell you where you went wrong?" Jessie knew, but couldn't speak.

The door to the office opened and in strode the lady, a newfound swagger in her step and confidence in her eye.

She said with hard voice that sounded like the female version of O.C.'s, "18.9%? On paper? Customer is ready to sign and you need to ask the boss?" Jessie didn't see the shot and was about to ask the lady what about the deal she didn't like when O.C.'s booming laugh shook the walls.

"Jessie, this here's my cousin, Latoya, and you just received some on-the-job training you ain't never gonna forget, son." He pulled a fat roll of green backs from his pocket and slapped a crisp fifty on the desk in front of Jessie.

"That's for doing everything right, up until the close. It's not what you would have made with the kill, but enough to give you a taste. You're ready, son."

That afternoon, Jessie sold his first car—an '04 Sentra for nineteen five at 24.9%. His commission was two hundred and twenty-seven bucks. He'd made in ninety-six minutes what would have taken sixteen lawns in the pounding Tampa sun to make with Mr. James. Jessie was the richest hustler on his block, and the cops would never shake him down. His gig was legal. He'd found a way to beat the system.

People in the neighborhood looked at Jessie differently since he'd become a success. Old man Roberts, who hadn't moved from the rocker on his stoop since Jessie was in middle school, gave him a daily nod each day before Jessie departed.

The shirt and tie were staples of a uniform that made Jessie feel important. Man's got to look the part to do business, O.C. says. O.C. had bought Jessie his first two shirts and a tie, fronting him the cash but making the aesthetic decisions himself on Jessie's behalf. You ain't no entertainer, O.C. says, you're a business man. One white shirt, one blue, one red silk tie which O.C. taught him how to tie on his first day on the job. Over, under, around, and through, O.C. said as they stood in front of a mirror and practiced the ritual. It's about respect, O.C. says. A man's got to respect himself before anyone else will.

Jessie liked the way he looked when he was dressed for work. At first, he saw himself as a young Denzel, but as the mornings came and went and Jessie needed but one attempt to get the tie to fall just below the belt like O.C. had taught him, he realized that no one in his family had ever put on a tie to go to work. When there was work to be had for his blood it was always the kind that puts knots in your back and grime under your fingernails. His family hadn't evolved much from slavery. They had been and were still mules for the man, but Jessie had broken the cycle. He used his mind to earn his pay. His body, which was young, was also hard, a genetic reward passed along by a bloodline of field hands. His body was his and no one else's. Each day as he knotted his tie and stared into his soul through his mirrored reflection, he added another layer of invincibility to the persona he'd created. If his ancestors could see him now, they'd break into song.

Great salesmen aren't born, O.C. says. They're made. That's because anyone can ride a streak. Luck finds all men, O.C. says. But it's what you do when your ass is on the far side of the sun that makes a man a success. Take football, O.C. says. These slick coaches with their million dollar salaries can add all the fancy X's and O's they want, but the game is still about blocking and tackling. Those are the fundamentals. They haven't changed since the days when the game was nothing but a bunch of slow white boys in striped shirts and leather helmets. Sales ain't no different, O.C. says. Guy starts to go wrong, he's lost his sense of the fundamentals. He's lost his S.E.E. He's not working the F.O.R.D.S. And he damn sure ain't working K.F.C.

I don't pay you, O.C. says. Your pay is in the customer's wallet. It's up to you to get it from him. And to do that, you got to build on the fundamentals.

Two minutes and not a word had been spoken between Jessie and Josiah. The air conditioning rumbled its BTU-infused white noise. The deal lay on the desk between them.

A sale is made every time, O.C. says. Either you sell the customer a car or the customer sells you on why he can't buy the car. Cars ain't weed, O.C. says. They ain't gonna sell themselves in this hood.

O.C. had sized Jessie right on the street two months earlier. Jessie thought his future boss and mentor looked like a cop in his pressed shirt and silk tie. "I ain't no cop, son," O.C. had said. "But you? You're a hustler. Nothing wrong with that except you're hustling in the wrong game." The game seemed just fine to Jessie. In two hours in the alley behind the Alpine Liquor Store, he could move a dozen dime bags and pocket fifty bucks. Fifty bucks before dark, not a bad supplement to the two seventy-five a week he pulled down cutting grass for Mr. James.

You can sling weed all day and all night, O.C. says, but how much green can you take? And what happens when you get pinched? And everybody gets pinched, son. Cops get you once, and you're a marked man. People get scared, they go somewhere else to buy what they used to buy from you. Next thing you know it takes twice as long to make the same green you used to make in two hours.

"You want something, mister?" Jessie had said. "If not, move along. I got business here." "

"Why should I buy from you?" O.C. had asked.

"Looks like you had a long-ass day," Jessie had said, "doing whatever you have to do in that tie. What I got will make you forget about the day shift and make your night open to possibilities."

Two sales were made that evening, even though money only changed hands for one. Jessie sold O.C. a dime bag of purple haze and O.C. sold Jessie on becoming a *real* salesman.

There must be about a dozen payday loan shops within a mile of O.C's on Nebraska Avenue. They're all mandatory stopping points on poverty's cycle, each offering a helping hand at a price that will hunt the victim down for life. The poor don't pay attention to interest rates. O.C. never said that, but Jessie had learned it all the same. Money isn't the root of all evil, insurmountable debt is.

To an outsider, O.C. may look like a car salesman, but he's really a bank. Caveat Emptor means sucker be warned. It's a lesson they don't teach in public school. The suckers moon in droves at O.C.'s. It's no different from how they gravitate to the alley behind the Alpine Liquor store, except at O.C.'s the swindling is legal.

A tear escaped Josiah's eye as he looked up at Jessie. The deal was for 41.9% and he was crying. "Trust in the Lord, and do good," Josiah said, before blessing Jessie and his family, "dwell in the land and befriend faithfulness. Psalm 37:3."

Jessie thought of the Bible verse about doing evil that may lead to good and how somehow that was alright. 41.9% was more than a kill. It was a slaughter. By the time the loan reached half of its term, Josiah will have nearly paid for the car twice. And he thinks he's getting a deal! He thinks he's finally caught a break.

There's a bus bench on the corner of Nebraska and Broad. Like most bus benches in Tampa, it's a billboard you sit on, a ground-level advertising platform with a message targeted at the locals. This one has a brother in a suit with a wad of cash in his hand and a game show host's smile on his face. *I want to buy your house!* the copy reads. Jessie used to give the bench a careful read each night when his shift in the alley was up and he had a wad of cash of his own in his pocket. He always thought that's what the better end of the hustle looks like. A nice suit. Respect from clients. So much cash that it only makes sense to invest. Most folks only saw a bus bench on that corner. Some saw an option. Jessie saw motivation.

He'd been part of the local economy since he was a kid. The hustling had started when Jessie was in the fourth grade when he would boost candy bars from the gas station on Sligh and sell them to his friends on the playground. For the last three years before coming to O.C.'s, he'd been sweating like a slave mowing rich folks' lawns for Mr. James. The alley behind the Alpine Liquor Store was a logical rung to climb on the hood's career ladder. Now he was legit and making a killing at O.C.'s. His picture would be on that bus bench before he was thirty.

People will tell you you're doing wrong, O.C. says. They'll point fingers on their way to the welfare office because they don't have the guts to stand on their own two feet and hustle for their own. They'll see the money you earn and they'll try to convince you that you're some kind of crook, O.C. says, but they got it wrong. We didn't have nothing to do with how the system was made. It's their rules, O.C. says, we've got to play by 'em just like everyone else. And you wait, O.C. says, won't be long before the same people who tried to bring you down are gonna come around asking for help. They'll come at you like the world is against them and you won the lottery—like it was luck that brought you that green, son. Worst thing you can do is give it to 'em, O.C. says. You want to know what keeps us down? It ain't drugs or drink. It's welfare, O.C. says. You give a man a meal when he's down, he gets strong enough to fight for his own. You give him a month's worth of meals, he gets full and lazy until next month when he comes back expecting you to give him more.

The first one to speak loses. Sooner or later, though, the man wants answers. Every male in Jessie's family had learned this truth through experience. The cop wants to know where you're headed. The judge will ask how you want to plead. Jessie's father had answered to the judge when Jessie was in diapers. Every year for the last nine he's answered the parole board's question of whether he feels rehabilitated and ready to contribute to society. Someday, Jessie knew, the white men on the parole board will grant his father freedom and he'll pick his old man up in a shiny Cadillac with leather seats. Someday.

Jessie could smell the close. 41.9%. Jesus, who else has the stones the slide paper with that kind of juice across a desk and sit back knowing it'll get signed? He was no longer a puppy fighting for scraps in a back alley. He was a wolf.

In a year, he would be ready to run this lot. In five, he could buy his own place on Florida Avenue. Not a *buy here pay here lot*, either, a legit dealership with genuine financing from a genuine lending institution. No more fighting for pebbles from the poor. When his time came, he'd sink his teeth into a higher class of customers who understood healthy debt was a path to the American dream. All he had to do was pay his dues, keep killing the poor and the door to the dream would open from the inside.

His was a neighborhood of lambs, of weak sisters who trusted God would reward their suffering in a kingdom that didn't keep credit scores. No man is a victim, O.C. says. A man makes choices and he lives by them. Life ain't nothing but one big sale, O.C. says. On any given day, either life buys from you or you buy from life. You look at the street, you can tell who did the selling and who did the buying, who did the negotiating and who took what came their way.

O.C. was right, but he'd left out the part about how the price isn't the same for everyone. He'd skipped the part about how some people take the bus to the market and show up hungry without a penny in their hand. Used to be the peddler would pity the poor, mostly because they were in no position to buy and would move on to more wealthy clientele. The poor would stay poor but no worse. We'd evolved. The peddlers had found a way to turn pity into profit. The poor paid their share with a lifetime of debt.

Jessie had lost track of how long he'd been sitting in silence waiting for the Josiah to sign. Long enough. He didn't say a word as took the pen from Josiah's hand, placed it atop the paperwork, and pulled the deal back to his side of the desk. It was almost four o'clock and he knew that behind O.C.'s closed office door his boss had his feet on his desk and was swimming in happy thoughts with his second glass of Crown Royal. O.C. wouldn't hear them leave, probably wouldn't even bother to look through the window and see Josiah and him hop the bus together. And if he did, Jessie would tell him on Monday that the deal for the Taurus had gone south, unless he landed a job on Florida Avenue before then.

Cracked

The bastard wore an Armani suit, fitting for a piece of shit who was moving up in the world and leaving unwanted baggage behind. I was wearing a terry cloth robe that bulged in all the wrong places. The robe didn't show my ass. I was doing that on my own.

The bastard held the front door open and Alec scurried through without making eye contact. The boy made a beeline to the Lexus, never once looking back over his Transformers backpack at me.

Fucking cunt rag.

The bastard didn't say it. Neither did the boy. I couldn't either. Somewhere in my brain there was a filter that kept the perverse thoughts and vile words safe from the outside world.

Too bad. An argument like this one could use some color.

My voice had cracked when moments earlier I'd unleashed a tirade, laced with just about every conjugation and variation of the f-word, all within ear shot of our eight-year-old son. No wonder why the boy didn't want to look into his mother's eyes. God knows what they must look like today.

"Get out!" It was the snappiest comeback I could muster, but at least I screamed it. My voice cracked again. The bastard smiled as he strolled from the house to the porch, closing the door behind him. It was a winning smile. A righteous smile. A you'll-hear-from-my-lawyer smile.

There was a mirror on the wall. I gave it a glance and wished it had Photoshop. My hair was thin. My eyes were red, and bulging from my skull. But this robe was a pathetic cloak. Who could win an argument wearing drab like this?

Make a scene for once in your feeble fucking life.

I saw myself march into the front yard. When the bastard refused to stop, I pulled the robe from my body, crumpled it into a ball and heaved it at the windshield of the retreating car. Standing naked as the day I was born next to the living wall (a green eyesore we'd dropped $17,000 on), I ended the conversation with a focussed rant about the skank the bastard was sleeping with and how I would own his ass in court. Even the neighbors sleeping one off could hear me.

He drove away without saying a word, because he figured that's what his lawyer would want. He knew I was digging in for a fight. The bastard knew.

I could feel the neighbors' eyes, peeking through the blinds of their overpriced homes at the train wreck standing butt-naked in the her manicured front lawn on a Tuesday morning, shouting perfectly woven tapestries of profanity, standing tall because she doesn't give a fuck.

That's right. Let those South Tampa hussies see a real badass.

I didn't ask to be this zip code's role model, but these prissy bitches, trying to keep their figures with daily doses of Vicodin and vodka, need someone like me to squawk about after their personal trainers cum on their backs.

Back to reality, where everything is so god damn safe.

I've never had the guts to make a real scene and this morning wasn't the day to break precedent. I never moved from the mirror. My eyes stayed locked onto my reflection as I heard the car backing from the driveway, chauffeuring my soon-to-be-ex husband and our son toward a better life. I stared into my own eyes until the car was gone, until the house was so quiet the ticking of the living room clock was the only soundtrack to my unravelling life.

Hurt someone. Anyone.

I threw my fist into the mirror. The impact unleashed heavy shards that fell to the tile. It was painless. Transcendence had vaulted me to a place where nothing hurt. And now my robe and the marble tiles we'd paid $57 a square foot for were stained with random patterns of blood. I'd clean the tiles, eventually.

Fuck the robe. It looks better with a sprinkle of self-loathing.

Nirvana tossed me back to the world after a few seconds of bliss, then my hand hurt like hell. I fell to the floor and let out a primal scream that was weeks overdue.

My purse had spilled its contents sometime during this morning's battle. I saw my keys on the floor and focused on the pepper spray canister attached to the key chain. The stuff had a rating that was five times stronger than what the government recommends to stop a bear attack.

What would it do to a person?

The urge to spray myself in the mouth took hold. When my throat jumped from my neck to escape the onslaught of pain, I would spray my eyes until they were runny eggs of mucus.

Drama queen. You know better.

A month ago, the bastard had asked nicely for a divorce. He used words like *irreconcilable* to describe our differences and *amicable* to paint a picture of how stress-free the proceedings would be and why there was no need to bring lawyers into the settlement. He'd convinced me I'd be taken care of and I'd nearly signed the papers that night. We were past the point of no return and a fresh start sounded like the right kind of cliche to get us both on track.

Then I looked through his phone and I saw her name: Yvette Cummings.

It was the most frequent name in his call history. It sounded familiar to me, maybe an executive we'd had over to dinner. I couldn't quite place her.

Googling her name brought all the pieces come together. Yvette Cummings was a divorce lawyer, the kind whose ubiquitous, melodramatic TV commercials made you want to puke.

Divorce is emotional. The details shouldn't be.

It was a tagline you couldn't escape in Tampa. Every time you saw it on TV, or a billboard, or a bus bench, you'd see Yvette's perfect face, with skin like a goddamn Barbie doll, breaking the fourth wall with eyes that said you could trust her to help you get through life's roughest spell.

Hire me and if I don't win, I'll suck you off to make up the difference.

The thing I hated most about her was her hair. She had a straight blonde mane that made her look like the head cheerleader in a Brat Pack flick from the 80's, the kind of perky teen who lived and learned in teen comedies, but was the first to go in slasher flicks.

I'd read everything the internet had on Yvette Cummings. She was from Tampa. Graduated from Plant High.

South Tampa rich bitch from way back.

She had a law degree from a school that was overrated, but she didn't flaunt her Ivy League education in her advertising. Her long legs and size-two frame were much more effective branding assets.

You'd love to string her up by her nipples and put her on display in a public square.

There was a certain comfort I felt lying on the floor of our home, crying uncontrollably amidst the blood and mirror bits.

This is rock bottom. Why does it feel so good?

I wondered if they called it *rock* because underneath the piles of lies and shit that made up your life there was a real foundation, a rock you could bleed on for a while before building yourself back up. I'd eventually start building. For now I just wanted to lie and bleed here, content that I'd hit my place where they say it can't get any worse.

Then the doorbell rang. The bastard was back.

I climbed to my feet and didn't bother retying my robe as I opened the door. Before I could say a word, I was transfixed by a set of deep blue eyes. This wasn't the bastard. This was a young black man with a body that was cut from stone and a face that belonged on one of those TV medical dramas.

"Hey," he said, "You're Melissa, right? Melissa Mucci?"

I made an effort to tie my robe without trying to be too obvious. "Mel," I answered, my voice raspy and spent from screaming. "People call me Mel."

"Right. Well, they put your mail in my box again."

He handed me an envelope. I grabbed it with my bloodied right hand without thinking. Instead I wondered how much of my body he'd seen.

He kept his smile and said, "You've been served. Have a nice day."

Dick move, but you liked it.

He added a whistle to his pep as he backed away and headed for the street. I slammed the door and fell back to my comfortable spot on the floor with the blood and mirror shards. It was safer down here, away from the world and judgement, away from all the social climbers trying to get ahead by stepping on the hearts of the survivors.

Quit being so sentimental. You're getting a divorce. Doesn't mean you can't get even.

My life was about to become an endless barrage of legal struggles: for alimony, for custody, for property, for sanity. I needed to find a lawyer. Not just any lawyer, one who could kick Yvette Cummings's ass. Where the hell would I even start? The bastard had always handled that kind of thing. Hell, he'd hired everyone from the lawn boy to the accountant.

My back was against the door. My knees were drawn to my chest, and I rocked slowly like a mental patient in a padded room. I was staring at a mountain of shit, and it was my job to clean a path uphill. Before I got started, I had to scream.

I let my body fall over, so I could stretch out on a bed of blood-soaked tile, spiked with mirror shards. Then I screamed. This one made the shards beneath me dance like they were being boiled. The tears came next, a sobbing that partnered with a good dose of hyperventilating. I was just starting to enjoy myself when there was another knock at the door.

I pulled myself to my knees, which was as far as I cared to rise before answering the call. I opened the door and the black man with the TV star looks peered down at me with his A-list eyes and said, "They say best place to be is between the second and third martini. How'd you like to join me there?"

❀ ❀ ❀ ❀ ❀

His name was Winston, but I didn't bother to ask until after he'd ordered the second round. We were the only ones in the bar, save for a silver-haired bartender whose lips moved as he read the sports section. It was just after 10 in the morning and the world was finally slowing to a speed I could handle. The vodka helped.

I stared at the papers I'd laid on the bar and weighted down with my keys. The can of pepper spray jutted back at me as if it were crying for attention.

Remember me?

I'd carried the can on my key chain since college. To be accurate, since Bryce MacAdams wanted more than I was willing to give in his dorm room in Castor hall during Freshman year.

Why don't you get out of the 90's and pack heat like a modern woman?

Women in South Tampa didn't keep perps at bay by spraying chemicals. They've got Sig Sauers in their Louis Vuittons. I'm not a gun person.

You like being the victim.

My pepper spray is like a rabbit's foot. Always carry it in plain sight and I'll be blessed with the luck of remaining attack-free. No action required.

You should've offered to blow Bryce MacAdams, then bitten his dick off.

"I wasn't at my best back there," I said.

Winston turned to me and said, "Everyone's got a front, no matter what's falling apart on the inside. Not you. You're a wreck and you're not afraid to let the world know you've bottomed out."

I processed the remark and wondered if it was a compliment.

"So this is rock bottom? I was wondering about that."

"Thing's will turn around. Most of the time they're not as bad as you think."

"My husband's sleeping with a lawyer."

"I take it you're not a lawyer," Winston replied with a grin.

"Until this morning, I was a wife and a mother."

"You're still a mother. Always will be. And until you sign those papers, you're still a wife."

"What about you?" I gave a half-glance at Winston, then brought my eyes back to my drink. He was wearing a Joseph Abboud olive plaid suit, the kind guys with Armani tastes wear until they can afford to dress like the big boys.

"You always serve people dressed like that?"

"You know what they say about dressing for the job you *want*."

"Don't tell me you want to be a lawyer, too. Just what the world needs."

"I *am* a lawyer. Divorce attorney, which means we have a common interest."

Bold.

"You serve me my papers, now you want to represent me. Check your textbook, counselor. I'm pretty sure that's illegal."

It's a play. And you like it.

"I didn't serve you your papers. The envelope is filled with blank printer paper."

For most of the morning, the envelope had been dismal drinking partner, a personal badge of failure. Now it was just a bundle of blank paper. I signaled the bartender for another round.

"Who are you?" I said.

"I told you. I'm a divorce attorney."

"What makes you think I want a divorce?"

"I don't have anything to do with the emotional part, Mel. My job is to make sure you get what you deserve, which in your case is a hefty payday."

"So that's it? My marriage is falling apart and you're the first lawyer to line up offering to suck my husband dry?"

"The law exists to protect you."

"Oh, is this the part where you tell me I'm the victim. Jesus, you guys are all the same. Pass the bar and you think you're God. News flash junior, I know lawyers with socks that cost more than *your* best suit."

Good line. You didn't quite deliver it, but good.

Winston smiled and said, "I know Yvette Cummings. She may not wear socks, but she's got a taste for expensive heels."

I couldn't help but cringe.

"Your husband hired her."

He did more than that.

Winston continued, "She's gonna be with him through the whole bitter thing. And right now —"

"She's fucking him."

"If you can prove that, this is going to be an easy win."

"Nothing's easy, Winston."

"Lot of angles to consider. I know 'em all, which makes me the lawyer you want in your corner."

"Yeah, why's that?"

Winston locked eyes with me and raised his glass.

"Like I said, we've got a common interest."

"Other than vodka?" I raised my glass just in case I liked his answer.

Clever.

Winston gave a sly pause then said, "Seeing Yvette Cummings come down a rung after getting her ass kicked in court."

We clicked glasses and tossed back the third round of the morning.

*****

Alec didn't size up the world looking for angles and advantages at every turn. When someone spoke to him, he listened with compassion and empathy. He didn't file a transcription of the conversation in his brain so that it could be later used to incriminate the speaker at an opportune moment.

Alec is a sucker.

When I casually dropped Yvette Cummings's name into an otherwise friendly chat, he had no idea that he was being used to gather information for my ulterior agenda. Alec was the last honest person I knew in the world.

And it makes you sick to your stomach that he's your son.

Eventually, Alec's naivety and virtuous personality would have to be curbed. If not, he'd probably get the shit kicked out of him for the rest of his life. Bullies would strip him naked and tie him up in the school courtyard. Girlfriends would cheat on him with the same guys who'd stripped him naked and tied him up in the school courtyard.

It was my job as a mother to toughen the kid up and prepare him for the world that doesn't give a shit if you're nice. He'd learn soon enough, someday. He's only eight years old.

I casually asked, "Have you met Daddy's friend, Yvette?"

Alec's attention was focused on a double scoop cone of rocky road ice cream when I dropped the question. We were in a Coldstone, which should have tipped the kid off that something was up, because I hadn't taken him to an ice cream shop in over a year.

Alec looked at me with lost eyes. Dapples of ice cream marked his nose and chin. He needed his mother, but didn't want to let his father down. A tough spot for a kid whose parents are headed for Splitsville. He only needed a little more coaxing to spill the truth.

The thought made me want to slit Yvette Cummings's throat and watch her bleed out. I could see my son standing in a strange apartment, outside the locked bedroom door while that bitch bounced on top of the bastard in an acrobatic sexual session that deserved its own website. I could hear his guttural moans and imagined I was in the room with them, a dried-up housewife strapped to a chair and forced to watch while wearing one of the flannel nightgowns the bastard loathed.

You always were a good little masochist.

Marriage hadn't outright killed my sex drive, but after giving birth and dealing with the chaos of motherhood, my libido blew away in a tornado of postpartum depression. The feelings of worthlessness lingered like a nagging cold and clung to my psyche long after the doctor cut into my stomach and pulled Alec from the coziness of my womb into the cruelty of the world.

I only needed to glance from time to time at the bastard's web history on his cell phone to reveal a lurid trail of porn sites, a not-so-subtle hint that he found me dull in the bedroom.

Tell them about the time you tried to spice things up.

The week before he would finally walk out for good, I had made an effort to give him the dirty carnality he craved. Alec was staying at a friend's house. We had the place to ourselves and could be as loud as we wanted, just like the old times. I made sure to leave tantalizing hints on the bastard's voice mail about what was to come in the perverse evening that lay ahead.

I had endured the torture of a Brazilian wax before heading home to prepare the bedroom for a night of debauchery. I was going to let him do whatever he wanted, and was sure to provide the required props for the occasion. Candles to douse me in scalding hot wax. Handcuffs to hold me in place. A ball gag to muffle my screaming. A blindfold to keep me from having to watch the whole thing.

The cherry on top was the outfit, a mail-ordered combination of red silk and lace that dug into my hips and ass and made me wonder if they'd sent me one that was two sizes small. I eyed myself in the mirror. Trashy which, given the bastard's internet history, was exactly how he liked his slaves.

The lair was set. I was dressed for the part. Now all that was left for me to do was wait.

The first text came at 8:29 pm. He was working late. I was coy with my initial responses, texting in the mindset of the sultry character I'd created. Sprinkling *hurry home, honey* messages with hints of what lay ahead. When my flirtatious wordplay went unanswered, I stepped up the game with a selfie that took thirteen attempts to frame. After hitting the send button, I leaned back in the bed and waited for the bastard to let me know he'd drop whatever work-related nonsense he was wrapped up in and come home immediately.

Four and a half hours later, I woke when I heard the front door open. I quickly relit the bedside candles then readied myself with a toss of my hair and a sprinkle of perfume on my cleavage, followed by my striking a rehearsed pose I had perfected earlier in the evening that included lying across the bed with one hand on my hip and the other holding my head. It was a posture I'd seen often while researching the bastard's favorite porn sites. I held the pose and waited for him to cross the threshold of the bedroom. My eyes focussed in anticipation of his face and the look of naughty surprise it would undoubtedly register upon seeing me dressed for his vulgar pleasure. I'd imagined his involuntary reaction and knew that it would be the height of my arousal in a night I had long decided was about him and his needs. I held the pose and waited.

Minutes passed. I called out, an inconspicuous *honey?* No answer.

On my way to the other end of the house, I pieced together a dialogue I believed could salvage the night. When I slowly opened the guest room door and saw the bastard had dug into the sheets and was snoring, my plans of seduction turned instantly to rage.

I thought about getting the .380 from the lockbox in the bedside table, and waking the bastard up by straddling him, sticking the barrel in his face, and cocking the hammer to the kill position just like the chick in that mob movie, the one who'd cracked when she found out her piece-of-shit gangster husband had a mistress.

Warming up to guns, I see.

I thought about cutting his dick off with a dull knife from the kitchen. Then I thought about doing both and wondered about the order of execution.

Castration first. Negotiation is more fun that way.

Come morning, he would try to say that he slept in the guest room because he'd gotten home so late and didn't want to wake me. I could see past his bullshit. The bastard had spent the night with Yvette Cummings. He'd drained his balls on her face and now slept the kind of slumber a man enjoys when his deepest needs are satisfied. Yvette Cummings needed to suffer.

The bastard needs to watch.

Alec, sweetie," I laid on an extra layer of compassion, "has your father had any friends over to his apartment lately?"

"No." His answer came too quickly.

"Alec, are you sure? It's OK, sweetie. I just want to make sure daddy's OK."

Alec dropped his eyes and stopped eating his ice cream.

"Alec," I ramped up her motherly voice, "has anyone been over to the apartment when you were there?"

No answer. I could see the shame in my son's wilting eyes.

If he keeps this up, you won't have to work up a fake cry.

"Dad says I'm not supposed to talk about family stuff when I'm with you."

The bastard already got to the kid.

"Alec...you know you can tell me. Remember who your mother cares about?"

Alec faintly nodded in a weak acknowledgment that he recalled the conversation we'd had about whose interests I held dear when it came to the family. I'd made the extra efforts in the recent weeks to convince Alec that I was on his side and could only hope I'd laid it thick enough to override whatever bullshit lies the bastard had fed him.

"Well, one night I had to go to the bathroom. So I tip-toed down the hall." Alec's voice was shaky. I willed myself to maintain maternal composure regardless of the story's outcome. "When I came out, I saw someone go from the kitchen to dad's bedroom."

"Who was it, sweetie? Who did you see?" I sounded like a cop who knew the answer.

"I don't know."

"Alec, was it Daddy? Did you see Daddy?"

"No. It wasn't Daddy. It was someone with long hair."

The boy dropped his eyes to the floor.

"It was a woman," he said in a shameful hush. "She was naked."

✿ ✿ ✿ ✿ ✿

The law offices of Cummings and Cummings were something out of a Carl Hiaasen novel, Florida charm in all the right places to divert attention from an underbelly of smut and greed. The building tried to pose as a home. A tin roof enveloped the storm-grey paneling. The doors and shutters were accented with teal. A wooden pelican wouldn't have been out of place on the wrap-around porch. It looked inviting, the kind of haven enjoyed by the well-adjusted.

This was a place that purported to put lives back together. I entered wanting to tear one apart.

I needed to see Yvette Cummings in person. I needed to force her skinny frame against the wall, look in her smug eyes, and tell her to stay the fuck away from my family. If not, I'd start a smear campaign on social media, letting the world know that Tampa's darling divorce lawyer was a home wrecker.

The words ran through my mind as I waited in the lobby and eyed the girl behind the desk. She was college-aged, with skin and hair that rode the flawless waves of youth. I could tell she was someone who met every day with a purpose.

Christ, not one of those.

No doubt she had what optimists refer to as a life plan. I felt like telling her this was as good as it got.

In a few years, she'd say yes to a guy with a big dick and bigger dreams. She'd have a few good years, maybe squeeze out a kid or two. Soon after, she'd slowly lose that tight body to motherhood, and someday find out her prince was sowing his royal oats with a younger, sportier skank in a Nebraska Avenue motel that rents rooms by the hour.

She'll learn soon enough.

Don't waste you hate on that bitch. You came here for a bigger fight.

Yvette Cummings was taller in person than she looked on TV. She was older, too. The maturity she gained offscreen gave her an air of professionalism. She looked credible. Her hair was even more annoying in person.

Yvette moved through the office with a commander's grace, then found my eyes and locked me down with a compassionate stare.

She knew exactly who I was, no introductions needed.

Her eyes were warm. It was an act she'd honed over years of bleeding people during their most broken hour.

"Hello, Mrs. Mucci," she said, without an inkling of ridicule. "Can I get you anything before we step into my office?"

After you, Miss Cunt Rag.

I had already thought of all the things I wanted to do to her. At the top of my list was grabbing her stupid blonde hair and emptying my can of pepper spray into her face. She'd kick and scream, but I wouldn't let go until her blood-soaked eyes were swollen shut. I'd leave her crying on the floor, then I'd stare down the college sweetheart behind the desk, daring the bitch to call the cops.

I knew better. These delusions would stay entombed in my mind, eternal cellmates with my inner monologue of perfectly crafted bile.

Pussy.

Yvette led me into her office, which had the requisite number of framed diplomas on the wall. She sat behind a desk whose sleek design looked expensive and ergonomically sound. On a bookcase was a picture of her in marathon-wear, posing at the finish line with her arm around some meathead in spandex. He looked like an asshole. I wondered if he had a wife who wanted to kill Yvette, too.

Yvette ran off a well-rehearsed spiel of legal banter about the bastard being her client and that he was determined to make sure I was taken care of. I stared right through her. All I could see was her bent over this desk, getting pounded by the man who'd vowed to stay with me 'till death do us part. The scene ran in my mind like one of Yvette's commercials, with the corny tagline playing over the money shot of the bastard draining his load on Yvette's Barbie doll face.

Divorce is emotional. The details shouldn't be.

I don't remember saying anything to Yvette, but I'm sure I muttered something polite. The next clear thought I had occurred when I was staring at a red Mercedes E300 in the parking lot. It had to be either Yvette's or the college bitch's.

Key that fucker. No one's watching.

I looked around to confirm I was alone. Then I snapped back to reality and locked the thought in my brain's cell with the others.

❊ ❊ ❊ ❊ ❊

Winston had advised against me going to the bastard's new apartment for a drink. He wasn't my lawyer, but he was getting there. For now his advice was sound and free.

Fuck logic. Even if it ends up costing you everything.

I knew the bastard wanted to talk divorce. Hell, he probably wanted me to sign the papers right then and there. But first, he'd invite me inside. I'd take in the place and look for flaws, but wouldn't find any. This was Harbour Island, and bastards like my husband didn't parachute from their marriages and land in fleabag shacks.

They land on their feet, in pussy pads like this, erections in hand.

He'd offer me a vodka tonic, and I'd accept even though I'd already had four before coming over. Then we'd sit down in his living room and talk like couples do. Maybe we'd reminisce about the old days and our first apartment together, a four hundred square foot den of hope near campus, where we'd spent entire days in bed and convinced each other no one had ever loved like us.

You guys did fuck like rabbits in that place.

I'm not sure what I needed or even wanted to hear. But what I couldn't bear to hear was that bitch's name. And the bastard wasted no time bringing her up.

Go ahead, call her a cunt rag, already. It feels great.

"Mel, I know how tough all this has been on you. It's been hell on me, too. But my lawyer says we can reach — "

"Yvette Cummings." I blurted it out like a middle-schooler who knows the answer before anyone else.

"Do you know Yvette? You've probably seen her billboards."

"Was she here? Tonight? In this apartment?"

He looked at me, obviously thrown by my question.

"N-no, Mel. She wasn't." Hesitation. Calculation. The bastard was working something over in that big brain of his. "But we've drawn up this." He produced a collection of papers. "Now, don't sign anything. Not tonight, anyway. Take some time with them. Go over them with your lawyer and — "

"I need to use the bathroom." I stood and took a step toward the hall, because this was the kind of place where the bathroom for guests is always down the hall.

"Sure, it's down the hall," he said. I changed course and headed for the staircase, my purse in hand.

"If you don't mind, can I use the one in the bedroom? It's a female thing."

"Go ahead. The bedroom's at the top of the stairs, end of the hall." Eleven years of marriage and the mere mention of the female menstruation cycle throws off the bastard's scent. Still, his answer came to soon, like he had nothing to hide.

He's hiding everything. But you're smarter.

I scanned the medicine cabinet in the master bathroom like an addict, desperate for a fix. Instead of a high, I was looking for clues that the bastard wasn't spending his nights alone.

Everything looked like it belonged. There was a Rogaine supply sufficiently depleted for this time of year. Edge shave gel with a white/blue crust on the can's top. A half used tube of the hair gel that I always hated. A dwindling bottle of the cologne that used to turn me on. It was as if he'd simply migrated his personals from the our home to his new life without skipping a beat.

The bathroom was so damn normal. Even the toilet paper hung the way I hated.

Don't puss-out now. Finish it.

A wave of vomit built in my throat and I considered emptying my stomach in the bathtub. I peeled open the shower curtain like Norman Bates and continued my hasty search for signs of female callers. The ledge against the diffused window held the bastard's Axe shower gel.

Wonder if he's trying to be like the kids in those the commercials who get attacked by co-ed sluts in heat.

Next to the Axe were bottles of Head and Shoulders shampoo and conditioner, his standard since before we were married. I was about to close the curtain, when the orange trim of a travel size bottle hiding behind the conditioner caught my eye. My cheeks flushed and my armpits moistened the way they did during a gruesome movie scene.

Pantene Pro V Ultimate 10 BB shampoo. Jackpot.

I felt the pride of a forensic officer at a murder scene that's been hastily cleaned to appear normal. You can't hide sin with Clorox.

If you were to hold a blacklight to the tub, you'd find traces of the cunt rag's pussy juice splattered on the porcelain.

The BB in the Pantene shampoo stood for *beauty boosting,* something the bastard would have no interest in; only a vain slut like Yvette, who probably sucked his cock and took it in the ass in this very shower, would use a product like that. I guess that's how she kept that blonde rug of hers in TV-ready business.

It was all the proof I needed. Alec was right. The bastard was fucking another woman.

❖ ❖ ❖ ❖ ❖

Tell them about the money.

The thing I haven't told you is that we're rich. Maybe you figured it out since by now you probably know I don't work and that the bastard must have deep pockets to own a house in South Tampa and rent an apartment on Harbour Island. There's more: stocks, boats, vacation homes, offshore accounts.

That's just the stuff you know about.

We're loaded, and after I sign the divorce papers, I'll still be loaded. Never-work-a-day-in-my-vodka-soaked-life loaded. Send-my-over-privileged-kid-to-over-privileged-schools-for-the-rest-of-his-over-privileged life rich. (That part earlier about Alec being stripped and tortured by Neanderthal-bullies because his dad raised him to be a pussy was just me being worked up and dramatic. The kid will probably grow up to be a pussy, but he'll spend his high school days being ignored by teenage coke whores and trust-fund affluenza cases with Porches. God, I love him.)

Keep telling yourself that.

The money doesn't matter.

If they don't believe you, they probably don't have any.

We didn't have any when we fell in love. Then we got married, had a baby, and the bastard got rich. So *we* got rich. What I did wasn't about the money. It had to do with me committing the best years of my life to a promise and having that promise stick its dick in another vagina. It's that simple.

She was in there. Somewhere in that apartment, Yvette Cummins was prancing around like a mare in heat with her perfect body and hair, driving the bastard into a frenzied ecstasy. I was sure of it. Yvette was inside and sooner or later she'd wrap that size four body around the bastard and grant him the fantasies I never could.

She'd let the bastard cum on her face because she was secure and sooner or later she'd take him to the shower where the fantasy would continue and after he had relieved himself all over her gym-toned ass, he'd fall asleep on his new bed and dream about hedge funds and dividends and whatever else got him off after he'd gotten off. That's when Yvette would be alone to cleanse her body of sin and debauchery. That's when Yvette would wash her hair.

❋ ❋ ❋ ❋ ❋

On my way home, I thought about Yvette in the shower. I pictured her running fingers through that long blonde hair, building a lather that she'd let sit for a spell. Then she'd wash it out, like she'd done a thousand times before.

This time will be different.

She'd step from the shower, rub a hole in the steamed mirror, and stare herself down. She'd be proud of herself for how far she'd risen, overlooking the fact that she was born with all the advantages. Her smug eyes would turn white with fear the moment she took a brush to that perfect blonde hair.

Flashing lights danced in my rear view mirror and bounced me out of my vision back to Kennedy Avenue, where I was about to be pulled over for a moving violation. At this time of night the cop would suspect I was driving under the influence. Guilty as charged. At least I knew who I'd use my one phone call on.

✿ ✿ ✿ ✿ ✿

The holding cell was a patchwork of uncelebrated Tampa bitches. The air reeked like the bathroom of a club at closing time on a Friday night. Of the quintet in the cell, I was the only bitch who didn't fit into an obvious stereotype. There were two hookers: one black with a skin-tight purple mini-skirt and platform heels that looked to be about eight inches tall, and one white who looked like she'd snorted one too many foul lines of coke at a Harbour Island masquerade. There was a rail-thin redneck with sunken eyes and craters on her face that would make a serious addict think twice about meth (she was probably the culprit behind the vomit in the corner of the cell, but I didn't have proof of that either). Finally there was Kasha.

Liking Kasha was less a choice for me than it was a lack of options. She was at least 220 pounds, most of it muscle, the kind of girl you wanted to make friends with on the first day of a prison sentence. Her ethnicity was hard to pinpoint. It was as if each of the Axis powers of World War II jerked a seed into a mortar cannon and launched the round into the uterus of whoever Kasha called mom.

She had the comfortably disheveled look of someone who'd been in the cell for a while, and by the way her giant frame dug into the cell bench, it seemed Kasha wasn't planning to go anywhere anytime soon.

"Man trouble," Kasha said, as she fixed me with a knowing glare from across the cell. "That's why you here. You one of them *scene makin'* white girls, be raising they voice when they man's been stickin' his meat where it don't belong."

I kept quiet. Kasha said all the things I wish I could say.

She's a damn poet.

"You aint gotta say nothing, girl. Aint nobody in here gonna listen, anyways. But I'm a say my piece. My man be gettin' his fuck on with some bitch from the block, bitch better be watchin' her back, 'cuz I'm fixing to monkey stomp her ass."

Monkey stomp.

It was a two-word phrase I had never heard in my sheltered life yet could discern its meaning by the way Kasha smiled when she said it. I felt myself grin for the first time of the day.

I listened with a glee I tried to hide as Kasha turned the cell into a personal stage for her one-perp stand up act. For the next forty-seven minutes, she wove a brilliant tapestry of obscenity-based ebonics in a rant that tackled every topic from the withering of family values to police brutality in the Bay area.

Kasha was a heavyweight poet, and I would have listened for the rest of the night. I didn't belong in South Tampa with the anorexic socialites and pill-popping soccer moms. These were my people.

"Melissa Mucci!" This from a raspy-voiced guard from outside the cell. "Your lawyer's here."

※ ※ ※ ※ ※

Three days later, we had lunch. A divorcing couple and their legal representatives sat down for a civilized meal at Jackson's Bistro. The place was the epicenter of South Tampa haughtiness, where the city's best-dressed elitists chug mimosas, gorge on filet mignon flatbreads, and congratulate themselves on being Masters of Tampa Bay.

They have no idea, do they?

Winston had told me Yvette Cummings had called the meeting and suggested a public place as opposed to a stuffy office. The aim was to keep the meeting cordial. I was in no mood for cordiality.

It was time I started playing the part of the damaged wife. Within the hour of being released from County, I had taken permanent residence in an Absolut bottle like an alcoholic-groundhog who wasn't ready to check on his shadow.

It's been three days. Sober up now and you'll never pull this off.

Winston looked professional. The bastard was calm. Yvette looked rattled. Her blonde hair was up in a bun that she hid in a trendy fedora that screamed whore-chic, somewhere between Ingrid Bergman and Cameron Diaz. Her hair looked darker, too —like it wasn't hers. It was a wig. My plan had worked.

Don't be obvious. Let her think you don't know.

The night I was arrested, I'd been at the bastard's apartment. So had Yvette, and I was about to get proof.

She'd walked right into my trap by washing her hair with shampoo I'd spiked with a Russian hair removal mix. It sounds crazy, doesn't it? Google it if you want to. Three-quarters of the internet may be porn-related, but the rest might as well be filled with sites dedicated to removing body hair. Dig deep enough, past the over-the-counter waxes and crack-job potions, and you'll find the serious mixes—the kind Russian prisons use when they're short on barbers and facing a lice breakout.

When I was in the bastard's bathroom, I emptied Yvette's beauty-boosting Pantene shampoo and filled the bottle with the stuff I'd ordered online. She'd spread it on that perfect head of hair like salt on a crop field.

Damn right. Cunt rag's head is like scorched earth.

It wouldn't be obvious right away. The first strands wouldn't fall out until after her hair had dried and she commenced her nightly combing ritual. Then, it would snap from her head like dried weeds from a bush. She'd run to a mirror with icy panic in her veins. Her blotchy scalp would stare back at her, yet she'd keep pulling strands, unable to stop.

Like scratching an itch until you're raw.

She'd pull her hair out until her transformation from blonde goddess to balding monster was complete. Then, she'd smash the mirror, unable to look at her own hideousness. She'd scream and the bastard would wake up. He'd see Yvette's bloody visage and wonder what disease she could have contracted.

You're the disease. But you already knew. Might as well own it.

The bastard had scratched me until my wounds became open sores, then he spread my infection to his cunt rag lover.

You won't do it.

Now it was time for me to reveal who they had to thank for Yvette's permanent new hairdo.

You're still a victim. Always will be.

I told you before that I didn't give a shit about the money.

You'll go to jail. There are rules. Last chance. This is where you normally pull up.

Prison was where I belonged, but that's not what I thought about as I jumped across the table and landed in Yvette's lap. As the cunt rag and I fell backward in her chair, I aimed my pepper spray at the bastard and fired a dose on his forehead. It was just enough to make him retreat, so Yvette and I could have a moment alone on the ground.

Holy shit. You're actually doing it. Atta girl.

Some good samaritan would separate us in a few seconds. Until then, I had all the time I needed. As I doused the cunt rag's face with pepper spray, I thought about all the times in my life I'd avoided physical confrontation.

See what I mean about striking first? No one can hurt you.

Hearing Yvette cry like a little bitch made me realize that guilt is a bullshit excuse for avoiding action. And consequence? Society has it backward. Living in South Tampa was my prison. For me, going to jail is like being paroled. I had awakened.

A-fucking-men.

I can't remember what I said to Yvette as I held her down and pepper sprayed her face until the fight left her writhing body. I remember thinking it was the greatest feeling of my life.

There will be others. Now finish this bitch.

Even as Winston wrapped his arms around me from behind and tried to yank me off the cunt rag, I remember thinking no matter what happens from here, it was all worth it. As Winston pulled me from the ground, I grabbed Yvette's fake ass hair and pulled. Revealing her scabby scalp to the world would show them what a whore gets for sleeping with a married man.

This part you'll want to remember. You've earned it.

It's funny what goes though your mind during a defining moment. As Yvette screamed and her hair remained in my death grip, firmly attached to her head, a sobering thought came rushing to me.

Maybe the bastard is fucking someone else.

The Exalted Cyclops

J.D. Schlocter had figured out why you were supposed to hate Negroes the first time his father showed him the postcard.

"You're old enough now, boy," his father had said when J.D. was eight. The boy followed as his father staggered into the garage, a trail of bourbon-breath in his wake. It was a Friday night, after all. J.D.'s old man was a good Christian on weeknights in those days, but come Friday he'd grown sick of reality, tired of breaking his back and bloodying his fingers at work whose pay never kept pace with the bills. On Fridays J.D.'s old man did what working men did. He went to the tavern and tossed a few back with the boys. Then he came home and cozied up with the bottle that lived under the utility sink in the garage.

J.D. never bothered his father when he was by himself in the garage on a Friday night. His mother said it was best. Over the years, she'd come to believe isolation was the safest way to let Fridays come and go.

That Friday night was the first J.D. had ever been invited into the garage by his father. The place was haunting, lit only by a single bulb. The tools mounted on the pegboard had jobs to do during the day. At night they stood silently in the shadows, witnesses to an imminent ritual whose uncertainty made J.D.'s heart race.

The boy looked up at his father. He was the biggest man J.D. had ever seen. The light splashed across one side of his father's face, leaving the other in darkness. The boy couldn't tell which comic book villain his father resembled—a farmer who was once good but had become possessed by the fallout of an alien disease.

His fixed his son with a glare.

"Once you're a man, there ain't no turning back."

J.D. didn't understand.

"You a man, boy?"

J.D. nodded and his father reached into a drawer and pulled out a small, rectangular piece of paper about the size of a baseball card. He handed it to J.D. and the boy accepted, never daring to break eye contact with his father.

"This is who you are, son."

J.D. broke from his father's gaze and looked at the card. He knew when he'd accepted the offering that it was old. Instinct told him to be delicate. He imagined he'd been given a flower as he held the card against the light to read the faded type on one side:

James Lawton. Jennings, GA 1912.

J.D. could feel his father's gaze, the same one he'd feel when he daydreamed in church. He was being judged. If he handed the card back now without examining the other side, he may never be invited back into the garage again. He'd disappoint. Worse, he'd be a disappointment.

J.D. took a shallow breath and turned the card over, then felt himself turn three shades whiter when he saw what was on the other side.

❖ ❖ ❖ ❖ ❖

Failure didn't bombard J.D. in a single calamitous swoop. It sneaked up and enveloped him over time, just as it had his father. The patriarch of the Schlocter family had instilled in his only son the values that had made America the greatest country on earth. Six days a week are devoted to work. The seventh belongs to the Lord. What's left in-between belongs to family.

J.D. never forgot the day his father took him downtown to the bank to see the man about a loan. It was a Tuesday, but father and son Schlocter were dressed in their Sunday best.

J.D.'s father stood tall and straight, even when the bald man with a splotch of mustard on his tie refused the loan, using words J.D. didn't understand. This was the Depression and times were tough. J.D., however, didn't think things were all that bad, especially in the bank, where everyone dressed like they were going to church.

J.D.'s father shook the man's hand and the Schlocters left the bank. They went fishing and J.D's father got drunk, even though it was a Tuesday.

J.D. had had better luck with the bank some years later when it was his turn to ask the man for a loan. Five thousand dollars was enough to buy the garage and open up shop. From sunup to sundown six days a week, J.D. worked in that garage until the grime took permanent residence in his fingernails.

His work made a difference. It was a calling J.D. took pride in answering. He kept the neighborhood vehicles on the road so his fellow working man could get to work during the week and take his family to church on Sundays.

Some years were better than others. There were times when J.D. could hire extra hands, and times when he had to let them go. Sometimes he had to work on Sunday, after church.

It never added up to J.D. how a hard-working man's paycheck could never keep up with his bills. In his perplexity, he was much like his father. The more he looked at his neighbors, the more he saw his own struggles. Somewhere along the way, America had changed its rules and rigged the outcome for guys like J.D. But it's hard to hate America. Still, a man has to have someone to blame.

✣ ✣ ✣ ✣ ✣

J.D. was working on Elmer Dudley's Falcon when he heard the roar of a Pontiac GTO as its V8 engine chugged at the light in front of his shop. No one in Jennings had a GTO, If anyone did, J.D. would know about it, so he peered from the garage to see who the driver was.

He took in the lines of the Pontiac, having only seen one like it in a magazine advertisement. It was the year the long-hairs had crashed the Democratic Convention in The Windy City, the first year of the GTO's second generation, the year Pontiac had redesigned its A-body line with a semi-fastback styling. The wheelbase had been shortened to 112 inches. The hood had dual scoops on either side of a bulge that extended from a protruding nose to the rear. It was beautiful.

The afternoon sun bounced off the endura paint finish and made the GTO glisten like it had just rolled off the assembly line. For a moment while J.D. admired the car, he felt the way good Christians should when standing in the presence of the Lord's more awe-inspiring creations: complete, contented, and in no way wanting for anything more than what's been given. Then J.D. saw the driver was a woman, a Negress at that, and cursed the Lord for leading him to believe the world was righteous.

❖ ❖ ❖ ❖ ❖

The picture on the card was a faded sepia tone. A group of people, mostly men, were gathered around an oak tree. Some stared at the camera, others paid it no mind. A black man hung from a rope tied to one of the tree's mighty branches. His limp body dangled like a dead cat in the jaws of a proud dog. His mouth was agape. His bright white eyes bulged from his head and reminded J.D. of the cartoons he'd seen that pointed fun at the dancing savages.

But the thing that stuck in J.D.'s mind wasn't the dead Negro, shocking as it had been to the eight-year-old. What J.D. couldn't shake from his mind was the woman in the picture, who looked as though she were exiting the frame having seen what she came to see and was off to take care of whatever responsibilities were hers. In her arms, she held a child of no more than two.

Even if he'd never looked at the card of James Lawton again, its image would forever be burned into J.D.'s memory.

❖ ❖ ❖ ❖ ❖

J.D.'s father didn't talk much at home, so as a boy, J.D. would save his questions for when they went fishing. He'd wait until they each had lines in the water and his father had taken at least three sips from his flask before he'd begin. He wanted to know who all those people were in the picture with James Lawton. J.D.'s father told him they were the men America had forgotten. When J.D. asked how a country can forget a man, his father said it happens all the time. A man breaks himself for America. He paves her roads. He fights in her army. Then he's turned away when his body's no good for work anymore and he can't earn enough money to keep his family warm in the winter. That's because there's always a new road to pave or war to fight and there's always a new wave of men lining up to be broken. America didn't hold up her end of the deal, J.D.'s father would say. He was usually drunk by the time he got to this part, but J.D. understood it as gospel all the same.

❊ ❊ ❊ ❊ ❊

The Jennings chapter of the Ku Klux Klan met every Monday night at J.D.'s garage. Most were already a few beers deep by the time they arrived.

J.D. peered from his office and took in the men. They were a spitting image of the forgotten lot his father had warned about. The decade may have changed, but the story had passed from one generation to the next.

They were the kind of guys who washed their hands in a utility sink after a day of honest work. Some had fought for America in Korea. Some had worked on the Interstate system that now connected one coast of the country to the other. They all looked weathered. Their bellies bulged. Their shoulders slumped. If his father could see them, he'd grimace at another wave of broken men, forgotten by the county they'd built.

J.D.'s father believed the Klan was the savior of white people. He said it was the only organization in the world that took care of white people and made sure they stayed superior. He'd been a loyal member right up until his heart attacked him when he was fifty-eight. J.D. had been with him when it happened. They were putting new brake pads on a Thunderbird that belonged to a lawyer. It was a Sunday.

J.D. never considered himself a poet. He wasn't much of a storyteller, either, as far as he was concerned. But when it came to passing on his father's rhetoric about broken men and a forgetful America, J.D. was well aware he had a preacher's gift.

The big difference between his father's day and his own was the place of the Negro. Order had been kept during his father's time. Now that order was falling apart. The Negro was coming up and taking his place among working white men. He earned wages just like a white man and even owned businesses that were, in some cases, more successful than his own. In fact, just the other day J.D. had seen a Negro in a new suit coming out of a bank with a briefcase in his hand and a smile on his face. That Negro had gotten a loan and now he was going to open a business and bring more Negro customers to Jennings's streets. Worse yet, he might make a few bucks and buy a home in a white neighborhoods and move his Negro family in. Wouldn't be long before there'd be a bunch of Negro families living among the whites, playing at the same parks white children play at, going to the same schools white children go to. Lord rue the day, J.D. lamented, when a Negro stands in front of the class as a teacher and poisons white children with inferior Negro thinking.

J.D. had learned that his speeches inspired more amens when he said *nigger* instead of Negro. So he did in the early days, and attendance at his meetings grew. It didn't take J.D. long to earn a reputation as a rabble-rouser, which meant it didn't take long for him to rise through the Klan's ranks: from member to chaplain, from chaplain to vice-president and from vice-president to president of the chapter—the Exalted Cyclops.

There had been a ceremony when J.D. became the Exalted Cyclops. Four robed Klansmen led him into a dim room, lit only by a burning cross. J.D. was told to kneel before the cross and promise to uphold the purity of the white race, fight communism, and protect white womanhood. After he'd taken his oath, the room erupted in applause. It was a big moment for J.D., who'd never been the center of attention of anything before. He'd worked his whole life without an ounce of fanfare, and now he was a part of something. Not just any part, he was the president of the Klan's Jennings chapter. He was the Exalted Cyclops.

✳ ✳ ✳ ✳ ✳

Jasper Sams died three months before the Irish president's brother was shot. There was a service at the Lattimore Funeral home, where all the Negroes in town were laid to rest. Most of the Negro community attended the wake, Mr. Sams having been somewhat of a pillar for many years on the dark side of town. He was the proprietor of Sams Barber Shop on 5th avenue, where all the Negro men went. Sams was more than just a place where men went for haircuts and to talk about baseball. It was, what J.D. came to learn, a cultural hub, a place where Negroes went to be in the company of other Negroes. What they talked about when they gathered each day, J.D. couldn't fathom. He'd see them, though, when he had to make a call on the East side of town and cutting through 5th avenue was the best route. Sams was always packed with Negroes carrying on and laughing like they didn't have a care in the world.

A block from Sams on 5th avenue was old man Williams's garage. J.D. tried to drive by the place about once a month to take a peek and see how business was going. Williams had been a jeep mechanic in the Great War. Now he was servicing his fellow Negroes' cars, which from the looks of it each month was tough sledding. Your average Negro didn't grow up with a car in his family, J.D. reasoned, so he can't change his own oil and the like. That's good news for old man Williams's business. Then again, how many Negroes had come up to a place where they could afford a car? If the old man weren't so old, J.D. thought, he might wake up one day to find he's in the right business at the right time.

J.D. didn't have to see the '68 GTO to know it had pulled into his station. He heard the rumble of the 400 cubic inch V8 as it approached from Main Street and gave three hearty roars that shook every tool box in the garage. J.D. knew the car didn't need a tune up. Somewhere between here and wherever the car was from, its tank had been filled with dirty fuel. He could tell by the way the engine chugged when it idled, but he wasn't going to say anything about it.

J.D. met the Negress driver in the lot by the tire display. She introduced herself as Beattie Sams and shook JD's hand. She had the looks of a Motown singer, the hands of someone who worked for living and the grip of someone who meant business, someone from out-of-town, not the least bit concerned that she was a Negress and he a white man. She said that she'd driven the GTO down from Nashville to tend to her now deceased father and J.D. offered his condolences. They weren't as sincere as what he might have given a white woman in the same situation, but they were condolences all the same.

Beattie leaned on the door of the GTO like she was in no hurry to get back to her side of town. She looked over the top of her sunglasses and said, "Old man Williams told me you were the guy in town to see about Pontiacs. Said you were the best."

J.D. had never been complimented by a Negro before. He gave an aw-shucks chuckle and said, "Guess you haven't had her that long, being she's brand new and all. Can you leave her for the afternoon?" Working on Negro cars wasn't his custom, but in this case, he'd make an exception.

"Actually, I was thinking about leaving her here for a bit longer," Beattie said. "How much will you give me for her?"

J.D. made the calculations in his head. The GTO sold for $3200 new. He could offer twenty-seven five, if he had it, which he didn't.

"Why you in such a hurry to get rid of her?" J.D. asked. He really wanted to know how a Negress ended up with a car like this in the first place.

"It's my brother's car," Beattie said. "Brand new. She's only got eight hundred miles on her."

"Still, though," J.D. stammered. "Why you wanna sell her?" He had a hunch the car was stolen but didn't know how to bring it up.

"This is a small enough town. You probably heard, but my father died and left his business in a spot. The place needs renovations and to do that I need cash. So it looks like what we have here is my loss turning out to be your gain."

Well, if this wasn't the damnedest day, J.D. thought. A down-on-her-luck Negress had come to him with a proposition and he didn't have enough money in the bank to make good.

"Your brother, huh? He's not gonna come around and try to take possession, is he?"

"Not likely," Beattie said. "He got drafted and they sent him to fight the communists in Vietnam."

J.D. pictured his firstborn, Jason, who'd graduated from Jennings Senior in June the previous year. The kid had a mechanic's gift and could give his old man a run on any engine that came through this garage. As father and son, they had plans for expansion. Maybe someday, J.D. liked to dream, when his hands were too old to crank socket wrenches, he'd let Jason take over. Wouldn't that be something his own father would've been proud of? But it wasn't to be, at least not for a while. A month after Jason got his diploma, the Army came calling. J.D. always believed it was honorable for a man to give his only son to serve his country, especially if it meant the boy would be defending the world from communism. He realized he and Beattie had something in common. Their blood was on the other side of the world fighting a war the heads on television say can't be won. The thought that his family's plight so closely resembled a nigger's heated J.D.'s blood like oil in an engine that was about to throw a rod.

❊ ❊ ❊ ❊ ❊

These were confusing times for the Jennings chapter of the Klan. A Negro doctor named King had whipped the country into a frenzy with his televised sermons about dreams and equality. His people were on the way up, and as far as the boys who met in J.D.'s garage each Monday could tell, were doing every bit as well as the whites.

"I saw a nigger today in a brand new GTO!" said Earl Berger, through a wad of chaw whose excess he liked to spit onto the floor as an oral exclamation point.

"Wasn't just a nigger," Dave Samuels said, his voice course with Lucky Strike residue, "was a damn woman. A woman!" Earl spat to add emphasis to Dave's point.

"You know what Pontiac stands for?" teased Joe Davis. Most of the boys knew the punchline, but they leaned in anticipation all the same. "Poor old nigger thinks it's a Cadillac." The boys erupted in a barroom chortle.

"Niggers are rising up, and we got our thumbs up our asses!" Keith Green said, bringing the room back to task. This time Earl's exclamatory spit landed on his own shoe.

J.D. took stock of the group. They were undereducated, underappreciated, and disillusioned, just like he was. They'd always taken comfort in knowing there was an underclass. Negroes had always seemed perfectly willing to play the part. Now they were getting uppity. The Jennings chapter of the Klan needed a fix of supremacy.

Throwing a brick through the Sams's living room window and letting the family open the door to a burning cross on the front lawn would send the right message. But J.D. couldn't see pulling off such an act so close to Mr. Sams's passing. It just wasn't Christian. Still, the boys were enraged, and J.D. knew if he didn't give them a release they were bound to light a fire neither he nor the law could control. They weren't organized enough to bomb a church, and they weren't devout enough to lynch anyone from the dark side of town. But they were drunk and they were hurting. They needed to feel the superiority of their fathers.

J.D. cleared his throat.

"Was a time when a nigger knew his place," J.D. said. The boys perked up like dogs at feeding time. "Wasn't the law that kept him in line. No, sir. It was order." A few grunts from the gallery confirmed the evangelist was striking a chord. "Niggers knew their place because lines were drawn. That's how our fathers kept order, and that's how we'll preserve the Lord's way. Standing together for the high spirit of America. The white men and white women of America joined *together* for the preservation of the ideals and institutions of the United States of America."

"Let us see the card!" Earl Berger yelled. He was out of chaw but spit on the floor anyway.

"Yeah, the card!" said another in the crowd. Scattered voices of affirmation came together and chanted in unison, "Card! Card! Card!"

J.D. held up his hand with the theatrics of a preacher at the climax of a tent revival performance. The boys quieted.

J.D. let the moment hang, then said, "It is the Lord's way, boys. He's chosen us to uphold the purity of the white race, fight communism, and protect white womanhood."

He held up the card of James Lawton and the boys leaned in for an awe-struck look as though it were a Bible autographed by an apostle.

❄ ❄ ❄ ❄ ❄

J.D. sat at the counter at Laura's Diner, sipping coffee and thinking about men on the moon. That's what the Irish president had promised by the decade's end and J.D. tried to convince himself it made sense. If Negroes could own homes and GTOs and do as well as whites here on earth, maybe space really was the frontier where his people would again assert their superiority.

He turned his thoughts back to Jennings where there was a real problem, and for the first time in a long while, J.D. wasn't sure of it being black and white. There'd always been an underclass in Jennings. Time was, you could find it as soon as you crossed 5th Avenue and the faces got darker and the lips got bigger. He wasn't so sure anymore.

Across the diner, he saw Jeffery Banks pick up a coffee and danish in a white to-go package. Banks wore a gray suit that made him look important, a man you could trust with your finances if you were the kind of man with enough money to hire someone to worry about your money. Banks was still a member of the Jennings chapter as far as J.D. knew, but he'd stayed away from the garage for some time. Lately, he'd made an effort to avoid J.D. altogether. Even at the diner, he didn't offer J.D.

so much as a good morning nod before grabbing his breakfast and heading off to business.

Banks wasn't the only uptowner who'd kept his distance from the garage. The lawyers, city councilmen, and others who loosened their ties after a day's work were too busy claiming their piece of the American pie to listen to a bunch of working-class stiffs air their grievances about the American dream gone wrong. For the first time in his life, J.D. wondered if there was a banker in the crowd among James Lawton. Then he wondered about the card and whether the wrong man was hanging from the tree.

❀ ❀ ❀ ❀ ❀

"I've got another proposition for you," Beattie sat on a dirty stool in the garage that Jim Saunders and his 300-pound frame usually favored on Monday nights. She leaned her slight body forward and J.D. listened to what she had to say.

"You need capital to upgrade every tool you've got in this shop," she said. "The time to do that is right now because there's a legion of customers just across 5th avenue who are ready to come across town because they know you're better. That's integration, in case you haven't heard. Black and white together makes green. Money is money, and I know you're short of it because you didn't buy my brother's GTO.

"My family's from Jennings," Beattie continued. "Came over on the slave ships and until recently haven't seen much change. We can thank Jim Crowe for that. My grandfather tried to make a change. He had this idea that the rich whites wanted to keep their place so they made sure the poor whites knew that niggers couldn't be trusted. Propaganda. Just like the Nazis used, stories to keep the masses in line. Problem is, people get to thinking a certain way and it's damn hard to undo. That's what my grandfather found out. He came to where the whites congregated and they beat him and strung him up to a tree."

J.D. felt a bead of sweat on his brow.

"Now, I'm not blaming you or anyone with peach-colored skin for what happened to my grandfather. It was a time when people in this town believed in stories. But I'm asking you, sir. Where has believing in that story gotten you? Has it helped your business grow?"

Beattie let the questions sink in.

"How many of Jennings's white sons have they sent to Vietnam to fight the communists?" she asked, then answered, her own question. "About the same number of black sons. And here we are back home, with a line drawn in our town that neither of us is willing to cross. Our boys are fighting for America on the other side of the world and we can't work together because we're too busy sleeping with one eye open. There's a ruling class in America, sir. And the greatest trick they've pulled is convincing the white man that black is a threat. We're all poor. And by we, I mean the poor blacks and the poor whites. *We're* the underclass. And unless we open our doors and sell to each other, the big man is going to set up his shop in our backyard and put us all under. He's betting we'll be too busy fighting each other to notice we're being invaded."

J.D. hadn't had a drink in twelve years, but he itched for one now. "What was his name, your grandfather?" he asked. Beattie's eyes lost their focus and dropped to the floor. Then, in a soft voice, she uttered a name that made J.D.'s stomach turn.

"Lawton. James Lawton."

❊ ❊ ❊ ❊ ❊

J.D. lay in his bed, unable to sleep. He thought about his son half a world away in Vietnam. Jason was probably awake, too. He may even be leaning against the back of a Negro, could be Beattie Sams's brother, two soldiers bonded by a duty to keep each other alive. Hopefully, Jason's mind wasn't heavy with moral conflict they way J.D.'s was. Hopefully, Jason was staying alert so he could return home to his mother. Please, Lord, J.D. thought. Let the boy come home to his mother.

J.D. wasn't much of a reader, other than the newspaper, but he recalled when the Irish president was killed some writer of prominence saying that maybe God doesn't care for America anymore. J.D. didn't understand then, but it made perfect sense now. America had done its share of malice on its way to superiority. The assassination was God's way of keeping the country humble.

His family had killed James Lawton. J.D. pulled out the card and studied it by the moonlight that sneaked past the window blinds and cast a ghastly light on a sinister scene.

The woman in the picture, the one carrying an infant and who looks like she's running from the camera, is J.D's grandmother. She's young in a way it's hard to imagine someone you've only known as old and broken. Her life is in front of her, yet it's obvious to J.D. that this moment, photographed and immortalized by J.D.'s grandfather, is one that haunted her then and continued its torment until her last day.

J.D. focussed on the boy his grandmother carried. The boy in the picture, like his mother, is blurry, an infant ghost who hurriedly passed through a sinister moment with no idea of its significance. J.D. felt a tear fall down his cheek as he realized he was holding the only picture of his father the man had ever allowed to exist.

As a boy, J.D. used to think his father had the power to see into the future. That admiration waned as J.D. grew and realized his father only ever talked about the past. Beattie Sams talked about the future, just as the Irish president had done before God chose to punish America, just as the Negro doctor was currently preaching a dream in which black and white live in harmony. Maybe, J.D. thought, a new voice had risen to lead America into the future.

❋ ❋ ❋ ❋ ❋

News of the Negro doctor's death found J.D. through the newspaper's front page. He was at his usual perch in Laura's Diner when he read the details, which J.D. took to mean God wasn't yet finished with America. It's the Lord's will, J.D. thought. It is He who strikes down black and white men leading the people to the future with a vision outside of His own.

Earl Berger burst through the front door. "Hey, everybody! There's a car on fire out there!" Earl couldn't help spitting on the diner's floor as the curious patrons stood and filed out of the front door. J.D. caught a glance from Earl, the look of a child trying to hide an inappropriate smile.

Smoke from the flames stretched to the top of the buildings on Lake Street and 5th Avenue. The onlooking crowd included most of the town, a gallery equal parts black and white. Everyone was concerned to unravel the burning mystery before them.

Two uniformed police officers kept the crowd at a safe distance from the flames, which engulfed the vehicle beyond recognition to most. J.D. knew whose car it was. He could make out the lines and parts of the endura paint finish that hadn't yet been burned. Yesterday it was a 1968 Pontiac GTO worthy of *Car and Driver's* front cover. Today it was burnt toast.

It would take the local fire department the better part of an hour to quell the flames. Most of the Negroes didn't stick around to see the charred corpse perched behind the wheel. None who did remain to see the sight cried foul. Husbands put their arms around their wives and walked home across 5th avenue without a word spoken to the white crowd who gossiped and pointed at the smoldering remnants.

A few flashbulbs popped and J.D. wondered if he and his fellow white onlookers were witnessing tomorrow's front page news. He'd seen all he needed. Glancing at his watch, J.D. realized it was time to go to work. There weren't any repairs scheduled for the day, but still, he needed to be at the garage because you never know who might stop by.

Your Trusted Reader

Dear Charlotte,

Thank you again for offering to read my latest work. As I believe I mentioned the other night at the reception, this is new territory for me—a real leap from the comfort zone I've been terrified to venture from, despite the admittedly stagnant nature of my career over the last several years.

Before I send over the passages in question, I want you to know that you will be the only living soul (other than me, of course) who has read these words. Not even my wife, who's critiqued every word I've written since college, has seen this. It's not the kind of subject she can approach with objectivity.

Every fiber of my being tells me that I'm utterly crackers for seeking feedback from someone about whom I know so little. Yet at the same time, I can't help but feel that our lack of personal familiarity makes you the ideal reader to judge these words.

I realize, however, this may be rather forward and I want you to understand that I would take no offense to your rescinding the offer to provide feedback if my divulgence makes you uncomfortable in any way.

Last chance to toss this letter and have us both go back to the comfort of unfamiliarity . . .

No?

OK, then. Here goes . . .

-Gerald

He had the Sirius tuned to one of those stations that play nothing but the kind of electro-muzak that was perfectly at home on the soundtrack of late night cable soft-core. His fingers danced through the woman's hair and down the nape of her neck. She tilted her head down and turned away from him, pulling her hair above her shoulders and exposing her bare back peeking from the curtains of her plunging evening dress. His fingers descended down the keys of her spine, gently fingering delicate notes along the way. When he reached her small, she turned her head to him, leaned into his torso and closed her eyes. He waited, because he had the power and knew every second he could hold her in suspense would pay off tenfold when he allowed her to release. He ran his fingers up her back and slid them inside her dress. That's when she took her free hand and latched it to the back of his head, so she could force his lips into hers.

She eased her grip when their lips met and he felt the warmth of her lipstick melting between them. This kiss was like a movie trailer, an intense preview of coming attractions. The only question in his mind was whether the show was opening tonight or was still another week away.

The back windows had become hazed with a light steam. He had a few lines prepared for when she'd ask if he wanted to come up. Play-it-cool lines, like Carey Grant would have used on Grace Kelly.

When the door opened she grabbed his tie and dragged him toward the night, relinquishing her grip just as she slid from the back seat to the sidewalk. Her suitor trailed at a pace he hoped didn't seem too eager, but was swift enough to minimize what he felt was an obvious erection.

On the one hand, he was proud of his tumescence, and that he'd achieved it naturally without the crutch of Viagra. On the other, he knew that time wasn't his ally. He'd left his little blue friend on the sink at his place and now hoped he could get to her apartment, where they could resume the action before any momentum was lost.

Once in the building, he quickened his pace to catch the elevator and leaped inside, just ahead of the closing doors. She pushed him into the corner and he wondered if he'd ever need Viagra again.

My first 400 words (or so). Too much?
-Gerald

Gerald,

If I'm not mistaken it was Twain who said there is no greater respect an author can pay his reader than to ask for notes on a work-in-progress. I'm honored and warmly accept your invitation to be your trusted reader.

I must say that I'm so far intrigued by the story's opening. The grit of the prose sets a cavalier tone in the tradition of the great pulp voices like Chandler and more recently, Elmore Leonard. Yet there is a vulnerability in this man, a reticence stemming from his insecurity that I find refreshing and charming. It makes me yearn for what's to come next, carnal or otherwise. (Hopefully carnal XOXO.)

I adore the anonymity with which you've cloaked your characters. We, the audience, don't know their names. I wonder if your characters do. Clearly, they're not interested in getting to know one another. Or perhaps they do and are role playing. Either way, the artistic choice keeps the energy focussed on the imminent passion, where it most certainly belongs.

My only suggestion is one of perspective. Suppose you employed a dual narration through which half the story was told in the man's voice, the other half in the woman's. Doing so would allow you to explore the male and female psyche with a freedom and subjectivity not normally associated with the omniscient, third-person narrator.

Your trusted reader,
Charlotte

For example, if I may, consider the woman's perspective where you left off in the elevator...

Teasing him was an option. I could have perched myself at the rear of the elevator and let him cool off until we reached my floor and retired to the confines of my apartment, where the ravaging would begin. Tempting, I thought, as I kissed him hard on mouth and forced him against the wall.

"What floor?" he asked, in between kisses. I could feel his manhood pulsing against me, the ultimate male tell. His was telling me I had complete control.

"What's your rush?" I said as I stroked his thigh and ran my fingers across the bulge behind his zipper, which shifted its attention and tried to follow my hand as it disappeared and traced a delicate line to the front of my bosom.

"I've got my driver waiting." He practically laughed when he said it. I thrust myself against him, pulling his hand away from the panel and toward me where it could be of more use. He pulled me into him as he leaned against the sidewall.

"Kid's got satellite radio," he said, "he can wait."

Steam from our writhing bodies rose to the flickering light above, then hovered among the wooden paneling where it lingered like a voyeuristic chandelier. The elevator remained motionless, doors closed waiting for instruction. Anyone could have opened them from the outside. Anyone, like Sylvia Barnes, who lived in 4B and was the building's resident gossip queen. What a story she'd have to spread among her piteous Friday night wine club if she were to discover us. The thought of being caught spiked the elevator's temperature another three degrees.

We were past the point of dialogue. He was the kind of man who knew when to shut his mouth and let the rest of his body take over. The air thickened with heat. I reached down and touched the number six on the panel, then brought my hand back to his tell, which was throbbing with lust and ready to attack.

Perspective. Have I gone too far?
Your trusted reader,
Charlotte

❀ ❀ ❀ ❀

Very well, Charlotte. Game on.

The elevator's doors slid open and she pulled me by the belt into the hallway. There, she pinned me against the wall and buried her tongue in my mouth. I barely heard even the slightest jingle as she slid her key into her door and unlocked it. She disappeared into the darkness of the apartment. I followed, not knowing what lay ahead but rock hard and up for anything.

The apartment was dark. I decided against turning on a light when I heard a match strike up and saw her lighting a candle in the living room, an invitation to follow into an unknown lair.

My walk was slow and deliberate, anything but eager. She waited until I was in arm's reach, then grabbed my tie and pulled me to her. Another kiss. This one more aggressive than before, as though we'd entered a new circle of lust. She grabbed my manhood through my pants, a habit I was getting used to, and wrestled my tongue with hers. Then she pushed me away, and I fell back to the couch with her in the middle of the living room, her own private stage.

Where would you take this, Charlotte? I give you license.
—*Gerald*

❖ ❖ ❖ ❖ ❖

He had a wife. Somewhere in suburbia, there was a woman sitting up in bed, reading Danielle Steel in a cotton nightshirt, with curlers in her hair, wishing she were young again, but thinking the world was otherwise fair. It turned me on, knowing that I was about to give him something the woman he'd sworn to stand beside until death do them part could not. I could make him feel like he was a master of the universe. Fantasy attained.

He knew it, too. There's no sensation for a man that can equal being in a woman's apartment and watching her strip.

Voyeurism is an aphrodisiac best served slowly. I turned away from him and let my dress fall to the floor. He couldn't help shifting on the couch, another tell that he liked what he saw. Of course, he did. I was as naked as the day I came into the world, except for the high platform stiletto heels and black lace panties, accessories Ancient kings would have demanded if only their concubines had access to Victoria's Secret.

With my back to him, I peeked over my bare shoulder. He was keeping his cool, which only inspired me to raise the stakes. I turned back to the couch and slowly crossed the room, taking short strides—one heel in front of the other—with my hands on my hips.

I bent down to him. He raised his chin to meet my kiss, but when he closed his eyes I grabbed the knot of his tie and halted his head in place. Then I pulled his tie from around his neck and threw it around mine like a sash.

He didn't say a word, but he smiled. That's when I dropped to my knees.

Your move.
Your trusted reader,
Charlotte

✣ ✣ ✣ ✣ ✣

I closed my eyes, leaned my head back, and let my mind go blank. My life had its problems. My daughter was marrying an asshole, my portfolio was having a shitty year, and my wife was on my ass to quit smoking. But none of that mattered, not then anyway.

She knew about my wife. I'd told her as part of the ground rules. It's important that we all know our place. Solidified status makes her try harder, and if there's one thing I've learned about these things it's that she likes it that way. She's good at being the other woman, the one with the figure, the femme fatale, the mistress. A rendezvous like this will eventually lead to diamonds, which will lead to vacations disguised as business trips, which will lead to an upgrade in apartment—all paid for. That's the game. Those are *her* rules, and who am I to change them?

Instinct and assumption can make a hubristic pair.
What do you think?
-Gerald

❄ ❄ ❄ ❄ ❄

Gerald,

I suppose you couldn't resist mixing a little misogyny with your illicit romance.

It's an interesting choice to halt a steamy scene in favor of a guilt-laced internal monologue. The only logical place to go from there is to have the man suppress his guilt by assigning roles and expectation (as you have). The woman is the harlot. The man is in control. His member will handle the moment, his bank account will take care of the rest.

In establishing such cliched machismo, you've unwittingly done something splendid. You've introduced a conjecture readers will take great delight in seeing never come to fruition, much to the man's demise. Rules are to be broken. Norms and mores to be obliterated in favor of lust. The genre demands it. The downfall will likely take place in the narrative's second act turn. Until then, let us return to the passion. It's where your readers prefer to be…

Your trusted reader,
Charlotte

He was almost ready.

A little gentle stroking with my tongue nearly rendered him unconscious. Another minute of this and it would be an early night for him.

I stood up, turned away from him, and leaned forward slightly. The next move was his.

And now?
Your trusted reader,
Charlotte

❅ ❅ ❅ ❅

Had my heart stopped in that moment I'd have considered it a good life and greeted St. Peter at the Pearly Gates with a wicked grin on my face. She had a heart shaped ass, and it was looking for attention. I pulled her slinky panties to the side and said hello with a kiss of my own.

She tasted like the first day of sunshine after a brutal winter. I let my fingers join the party and soon it was my turn to be the one driving her to the brink of ecstasy. If she had neighbors, they were surely reaching for their ear plugs by now. If her moans in the early innings were any indication, it was going to be a loud night.

I like where this is going.
How about you?
-Gerald

❖ ❖ ❖ ❖ ❖

Dear Mr. Powell,

It is with the heaviest of hearts that I write you to inform that my mother, Charlotte Mayhew, passed away on Monday after a long battle with several illnesses. In her final days, Mom spoke fondly of you and the friendship you two had developed while exchanging letters over the last few months. I can't tell you how wonderful it was to see her happy.

I understand you live at Cinnamon Oaks as well. I'm not sure how social Mom allowed herself to be there, which is why it's simply splendid that you and she connected, especially via letter. For years I was convinced my mom was the last letter writer on earth. She saw the telephone as a necessary evil, but wouldn't extend the courtesy to email. (Don't even ask about cell phones and text messaging.) She loved writing letters, almost as much as she loved lying about her age. Mom always took pride in her deftness at both endeavors.

Mom wanted you to have the letters you exchanged, and so I've included them--sealed and to be read only by you, as was her wish.

I'm afraid I'm not the artist with words that Mom was, which is why I've always found it best to simply say *thanks* when someone does something wonderful for you or someone you love. On behalf of my mother, thank you for your kindness and friendship.

Sincerely,
Dr. Lindsey Foster, M.D., F.A.A.D.

P.S. Mom was eighty-six. (But, you didn't hear it from me.)

Pencil Fight Club

DATE: SEPTEMBER 6, 1987
FROM: HEADMISTRESS GAVEL
TO: ALL TEACHERS
RE: PENCIL FIGHTING

EFFECTIVE IMMEDIATELY, ANY STUDENT CAUGHT 'PENCIL FIGHTING' ON SCHOOL GROUNDS IS TO BE BROUGHT DIRECTLY TO MY OFFICE. DO NOT ATTEMPT TO DISCIPLINE VIOLATORS YOURSELF.

As pop-fad games go, pencil fighting should rank with pick-up sticks and paper football—enrapturing scholastic distractions from a simpler time the Snapchat generation will never know.

Back in the day of Rubik's Cubes and Choose Your Own Adventure books, pencil fighting was the guiltiest of all elementary school pleasures. It was a contest of skill enjoyed by classroom deviants and wannabe outlaws like yours truly and my fourth-grade gang of private school bandits.

Take Eli Haber. For the entire month of April in 1986 "The Slam from Beth Am" had a first-lick knockout percentage of

57%, an incomparable stat that would have been higher if it weren't for Stephan Schneider's keen ability to psyche Eli out with a never-ending barrage of pre-lick trash talk about his unapproachable crush, sixth-grader Rachel Zelnick.

And who could forget Ricardo "The Rock" Arboleda, whose nickname stemmed from pencils ability to take a lick after lick without breaking.

To a ten-year-old boy, there is no greater feeling than to grip a #2 pencil, pull back on its eraser end, whip down on your opponent's outstretched pencil and slice it in half. Of course, the shame of defeat is equally as cathartic as the elation of victory. Feeling every wood and graphite fiber in your pencil sever and watching your victorious opponent gloat like a Roman gladiator is far more humbling and humiliating than taking a dodgeball to the face. I would know.

In my young elementary school career, I had witnessed pencil fights last more than ten savage rounds. Who could forget the time Steven Reynolds outlasted Chris Feldman in a slugfest that went twenty-three licks a piece? By the end of the fight, both fighters were soaked in sweat, nerves shot. Each looked like he'd gone the distance with Rocky Balboa. It was the kind of storied battle that fueled our lunchtime and recess talks for a year.

Beloved as our favorite pastime was, pencil fighting was officially banned at Hamilton Elementary in the Fall of 1987. The law was passed on the second day of my fourth-grade year when Doctor Gavel halted a fight between Nicholas Pfizer and me in the cafeteria. The edict was delivered in front of an audience of fourteen pre-pubescent boys and Sarah Casey, a fellow fourth-grader and tomboy who preferred the action of a good pencil fight to the girly gossip of her fellow coeds.

On that fateful day, the Headmistress of our school and most feared private-school educator in the district gathered every boy in the cafeteria along with Sarah and explained the dangerous nature of our favorite past time. It was like being dressed down by Darth Vader. Cold sweat trembled on my ten-year-old brow and I wondered if at any moment I might be choked by an invisible hand. *Doctor* Gavel, as our school's Headmistress, commanded students her call her, presented a compelling case for the needless risks pencil fighting presented.

While the odds of a wood shard finding our exposed pupils seemed long if not astronomical, Dr. Gavel made it painstakingly clear she would not condone the pointless destruction of pencils — tools, she asserted, existed for creation not destruction.

And so it came to be during the first week of my fourth-grade year that pencil fighting at Hamilton Elementary went the route of gum chewing and card playing, a gleeful act that would forever be frowned upon and punishable with a trip to the Headmistress's office and a phone call home.

Pencil fighting, our most beloved of all indoor sports, the thing that set the social pecking order of boys at Hamilton Elementary, was made to be a crime whose accessories were considered public enemy number one by the ruling administration.

None of us dared challenge the iron-clad rule, until a new kid named Eddie Castillo transferred to Hamilton.

No one knew for sure where Eddie was from or how he ended up in our class. He had been at a public school, which for us meant he was the closest thing to a convict we'd ever seen in real life. Allison Bergeron heard from her older sister that Eddie had been arrested for stealing cigarettes from a vending machine. Tynan "Time Bomb" Baumgartner affirmed the rumor, but heard from a kid in his karate class that arrest had nothing to do with stolen cigarettes and could best be described as gang-related. Louis Diego, whose father was an FBI consultant, swore that Eddie had been held back a year because he'd been in the bureau's witness protection program.

Regardless of his elusive origin, Eddie needed less than a week to take pencil fighting at Hamilton underground, where it could thrive as the brutal death sport it would soon become.

The boys bathroom near the janitor's closet was the perfect lair for our illicit pencil fighting ring. It was far enough away from Dr. Gavel's office and offered a clear view of the only way in, should she or any other teachers try to catch us in the act.

The bathroom quickly took on the unspoken code of Prohibition-era speakeasy. We assigned lookouts who warned of approaching faculty with enough time for us to transform the place from a den of illegal activity back to its innocuous self. Teachers were always suspicious and occasionally tried to coerce weaker-willed kids (like me) into spilling the beans about our pencil fight club. But no one ever talked. The fear of Eddie kept us in line.

He had earned the nickname "One Lick Eddie" when he disposed of his first eleven pencil fighting opponents at Hamilton with one lick a piece. His early contests showed the skill of a determined prize fighter tenaciously rising through the ranks on a collision course with the championship belt. Along the way, he had amassed a highlight reel of knockout blows, including a first lick knock out of Kenny "Softer-than-Butter" Parkay that Eddie executed *with his eyes closed*.

Graphite trembled in his opponents' hands while they waited for Eddie's mighty lick that needed but one chance to cut his challenger's pencil in half. His flawless technique turned his pencil into a battle ax. Against him, the rest of us might as well have held microwaved string cheese.

He was the greatest any of us had ever seen. A man among boys. An artist among journeymen. A god among mortals.

Eddie was the best, and he knew it.

The only thing at Hamilton that could rival One Lick Eddie's skills was his mouth. When it came to verbal taunting, Eddie was the undisputed king, a purveyor of elite trash talk who could've held his own on a basketball court in the prison system. He was particularly deft at spewing an endless string of phallic references that, despite our pre-pubescent inexperience, rattled our sporting brains with empty feelings of inadequacy.

Most fights with Eddie were over *before* the first lick. A master of the head game, he took sadistic pleasure in toying with the minds of his challengers. His devastating brand of psychological warfare could crush the will of any adversary lacking profound mental fortitude.

I was crazy to challenge him.

It was Sarah Casey's idea. When our fighting ring sought refuge in the boys' bathroom, Sarah became a reluctant outsider, forced to play the role of lookout instead of spectator. She would find me the moment a fight ended and unleash a barrage of enthusiastic questions. Who won? How many licks? What kind of techniques were used? It was as though Sarah was filing away an endless spreadsheet of stats and metrics in her head, a freaky skill that proved a useful resource when the particulars of a past fight were in dispute during a passionate war story exchange at lunchtime.

Sarah and I had been friends since kindergarten. We grew up chasing each other on Big Wheels, then graduated to bikes and skateboards. Fourth grade was shaping up to be a tough social year for Sarah. The girls didn't accept her and none of the boys would dare pencil fight her. There's nothing to be gained by fighting a girl. If you win, you've simply beaten a girl. And if you lose…

Despite her inability to procure a match, Sarah loved pencil fighting. Whenever she and I were alone, she would overload me with talk of techniques for both offense and defense. Her scientific approach to the sport fueled her spouting of theoretical terms like strike angle, torque output, thumb pressure, and pounds per square pencil inch.

Though I didn't understand a word of it, I listened to Sarah and indulged her endless breakdowns of technical prowess, realizing that it was her way of coping with being a pariah in a segregated sport.

She had every boy in our class broken down like a seasoned sabermetrician. According to Sarah, Eli Haber's strike angle varied three to seven degrees from his first lick to second, which accounted for a significant drop in his knockout rate after the first lick. Nicolas Pfizer's torque output was among the highest in the class. Unfortunately for him, so too was his thumb pressure to torque ratio, an imbalance that resulted in Nicolas's high rate of *self-inflicted* knockouts whereby the striker's pencil breaks while taking a lick. One Lick Eddie, in contrast to the rest of our class, possessed all the elements of a perfect strike in ideal harmony that resulted in a blow whose pounds-per-square-pencil inch were optimized to achieve maximum lethalness.

You can take him.

I knew what the cryptic note meant as soon as Sarah slid it to me during Mrs. Sternbaum's lesson on prepositions. I just didn't believe it myself.

Sarah persisted for the balance of the day, trying to persuade me to challenge Eddie to a fight. Years later I would come to admire her pleading, but in my fourth-grade mind, I could think only of the shame I'd feel when my pencil sliced in two upon bearing the brunt of Eddie's wicked lick.

Realizing her pitch was falling on deaf ears, Sarah intensified her hard-sell tactics during lunch. She fed me my stats for the year. My record was respectable. Seventeen wins against only six defeats. Sarah pointed out that two of my losses had come by way of self-inflicted knockout. She also harped on the truth that eight of my seventeen wins had come by way of a first-lick knockout. Eight, according to Sarah's stat keeping, ranked me second in the class for the category. Atop the list was, of course, Eddie, whose intimidating record was an unblemished 36-0, with 33 of his wins by way of first lick knockout.

I glanced across the cafeteria and saw Eddie holding court with a quartet of sixth-grade girls, including Hanna Vanderspool, whom I'd secretly had a crush on since the second grade. Sarah knew about my fawning over Hanna. When we weren't talking about pencil fighting, she indulged my gabbing about the girl who since the first grade had been the star of her father's perpetually running TV commercials for his jewelry store. Rumors on the playground during recess hinted at her being cast in an upcoming Nickelodeon show.

What was no rumor was the fact that Hanna hung on One Lick Eddie's every move. Of course, she liked him, Sarah pointed out. Eddie was the bad boy who rode his bike to school. Not just any bike, either—a Mongoose Californian with Pro Class bars and rims. He knew the lyrics to every Beastie Boys song and was rarely knocked out in dodgeball. But most importantly, he was Hamilton's undisputed champion of pencil fighting. Girls like Hanna liked winners. By the end of lunch, Sarah had connected the dots. If I beat Eddie, Hanna would take notice.

The actual moment I challenged the champion of Hamilton Elementary to a pencil fight can best be described as an out-of-body experience. I remember walking across the cafeteria, my Nikes getting heavier with each step that brought me closer to Eddie. My head was on fire and thick beads of sweat flooded the pores of my face that weren't already clogged with pimples. My voice reverted to its first-grade squeak when I asked Eddie if he was *available* after school for a fight. Out of the corner of my eye, I could see Hanna looking at me. Her gaze was like a heat lamp that made me long for the sub-freezing temperature of Señor Valderama's Spanish Class. Our eyes met, and for the briefest of moments she smiled. My fleeting elation ended the moment Eddie accepted my challenge and told me I should bring a pizza to the fight in case he got hungry after humiliating me. "On second thought," he said, "don't bother. I'll just eat your face instead."

I don't remember walking away and returning to the other side of the cafeteria. But I do remember Sarah encouraging me to focus on the only thing that mattered: I had a shot at the title. Three o'clock high in the boy's bathroom near the janitor's closet.

A date with destiny. An appointment with the undertaker. A sentence by the executioner.

I was going to be sick.

I spent most of the hours between lunch and the three o'clock bell conjuring ways I could honorably postpone the fight. Catching my thumb in a door seemed a practical way to sustain an injury that would excuse me from fighting. Then again, a strategically placed paper cut would accomplish the same debilitating affliction while providing physical proof to keep me from being called a faker.

Sarah wouldn't hear it. She said I was crazy to even think about backing down from what was clearly the defining moment of my young scholastic career. She knew I could beat Eddie and would stop at nothing until I believed it myself.

You can take him.

The words became a mantra Sarah repeated to me right up until the three o'clock bell rang like an alarm from the emergency broadcast system. Our class dispersed with most of the boys making their way to bathroom where the main event would take place. I caught a glimpse of Hanna Vanderspool in time to catch her laughing at another of Eddie's jokes. That's when the champion's eyes locked onto mine and he mouthed the words that made me wish I was home with the flu.

You're dead.

I made the slow walk to the boy's bathroom by the janitor's closet with Sarah offering words of encouragement like machine gun fire.

Block out his trash talking.

See his pencil breaking into pieces.

Follow through on every stroke.

Focus.

We stopped just before the door to the boys bathroom. This was the end of the line for Sarah, and as I took a deep breath before entering, my lone supporter offered one final encouragement:

You can take him.

She believed it. I didn't, but I went in anyway.

The bathroom was eerily quiet when I entered. The usual pimple-faced crowd stared at me with an equal mix of awe and pity. Then the door opened and One Lick Eddie entered the ring like Mike Tyson at Caesar's Palace. I half expected there to be smoke and an entourage of vaguely familiar rappers holding his robe. He was alone, but all business, and wore the game face of fighter poised to finish me off quickly.

My plan of attack rested on me getting first lick, which meant I needed to win the pre-fight game of rock-paper-scissors. I had sized up Eddie to be a rock guy. Anyone with such devastating pencil fighter skills had to be a rock guy, but Sarah had metrics that proved otherwise. In fourteen rock-paper-scissors contests this year, Eddie had gone with scissors a surprising eleven times.

She had urged me to play the percentages if it came down to it. Now, here we were.

One.

He's got to be a rock.

Two.

Paper. I'm ready with paper.

Three…

But what if Sarah's right?

Shoot!

The crowd looked in for several tense beats of silence as everyone assessed the results. Eddie held out his two fingers. Scissors. I held out my fist. Rock.

The first lick was mine.

As I took my warm-up licks, Eddie confessed the real reason he was at Hamilton. He'd been expelled from his last school for pencil fighting after slicing a pencil with such devastation that a piece of mangled wood jettisoned from the wreckage and found the loser's eye. The kid Eddie had beaten wore an eye patch for the rest of the year. Now, Eddie was going to do the same to me. I did my best to tune out his bile, focussing only on following through and seeing his pencil shatter in two. But I couldn't stop his words from getting into my head.

I tried to recall Sarah's sage advice:

Block out his trash talking.

See his pencil breaking into pieces.

Follow through on every stroke.

Focus.

I cocked my #2 American Faber Castell and unleashed it on Eddie with every ounce of ferocity I could muster. It felt powerful. It felt pure. It bounced off of Eddie's pencil without inflicting so much as a dent.

Eddie cracked a wicked grin. I knew there was no sense in delaying the inevitable. I held my pencil for him to take his lick, wondering if I should close my eyes for safety or keep them open so I could watch the master at work. I just hoped it would be over quickly.

And it was.

True to his nickname, Eddie disposed of me in a single lick, upping his record to 37-0. The winner by knockout and still-undefeated champion of Hamilton Elementary gloated his win and taunted the onlooking crowd like Achilles before an army of thousands, daring anyone brave (or stupid) enough to challenge him or forever remain in cowardly silence.

A lone challenger emerged, not from the crowd who had just witnessed my humiliating defeat, but from the door. We looked in utter shock as the contender entered the boy's bathroom, crossed the linoleum floor and stood toe-to-toe with the champion.

Sarah.

It was likely the first time in the history of Hamilton Elementary that a girl had set foot in the boy's bathroom, and definitely the first time a girl had stepped into a pencil fight since our ring was forced underground. Yet Sarah was undaunted. She eyed the reigning champion like a hungry contender with her sights on the title.

Eddie laughed off her challenge. A girl wasn't worthy of fighting him, even if this one had risked an in-school suspension and endured smells no fourth-grade coed should ever experience. He was three steps toward the door when Sarah called him back to the ring with the mocking sound effect of a cackling chicken. That's when the champion did an about-face and returned with a look of hatred in his eyes. He readied himself for rock-paper-scissors. This time, Eddie would vary his predictable pattern. Or would he? The psychological game within a game was on.

Sarah held up her hand before the contest began. The gallery let out a noticeable gasp. She was giving him first lick! No one had conceded first lick in the recorded history of pencil fighting at Hamilton. Yet here Sarah was, deferring the opening blow to One Lick Eddie, who was a shocked as the rest of us at the tactic.

Sarah held her pencil for Eddie to size up. He cocked his instrument of death and let it fly with a vengeance. His pencil's sweet spot landed with a mighty clack that reverberated throughout the bathroom, but it didn't break Sarah's pencil.

She was still alive.

Sarah smiled as she motioned for Eddie to ready himself for her return fire. The champion was as surprised as us that Sarah was still in the fight. Her pencil must have suffered internal damage and would surely break in her hands as she attempted her lick. It would be a self-inflicted knockout but could be considered a moral victory, especially for a girl.

I could see in Sarah's eyes that she didn't cross the line of decency and come to the boy's bathroom for a moral victory. She was out for blood. Her practice licks showed the will of a long shot who believed the championship belt was within reach.

One good lick. That's all she needed. That's when I vocalized my belief and openly endorsed Sarah.

You can take him.

Sarah's eyes found mine and, in a moment I've never forgotten, she winked at me. Eddie went for the jugular with a nasty line of trash about Sarah's ineptitude with hard wood in her hands. She set her feet, lowered Eddie's pencil into her striking zone, stared the champion in the eye, and smiled. T h e n she let loose the most legendary lick ever taken in the history of pencil fighting at Hamilton Elementary.

Eddie's pencil sliced in two, but that wasn't the reason that decades later this story remains so vivid in my mind and in the minds of all the pre-teen private school boys who were in the bathroom that day. A shard of wood launched from Eddie's shattered pencil and landed in his eye, causing him to double over. The champion who'd terrorized our school with a reign of trash talking and ruthless licks began whimpering like a toddler. He stumbled out of the bathroom in tears, leaving us to mob our new champion with cheers that could surely be heard in Dr.

Gavel's office. We didn't care. There was a new pencil fighting champion at Hamilton Elementary.

A legend had been born.

Eddie Castillo transferred from Hamilton Elementary the next week. There was much speculation as to where the former champ went or what stories he would tell his new classmates when he got there. Most of us, however, wondered how long he would have to wear an eye patch at his new school.

In the wake of Eddie's departure, pencil fighting at Hamilton was not only permanently banned but upgraded in punishment with perpetrators serving a weeklong in-school suspension in Dr. Gavel's office.

Sarah Casey, who would go on to earn a PhD in structural engineering from MIT, never participated in another pencil fight again. Her official record in 1987 would remain 1-0, with her lone win by way of the most memorable knockout the sport has ever seen.

It was just as well that our days of pencil fighting at Hamilton were over. None of us would have ever beaten her.

Sammy's Wilson's Last Christmas

My tear ducts are no match for the Christmas card Sammy Wilson gave me when he was five years old. Every Christmas Eve, it's the same routine. My family gathers in the living room. I make a big show of the card as I build up to my annual telling of the Christmas story you're about to hear.

Every year, I tear up before I can get through the story's opening act.

Sammy gave handmade Christmas cards to the entire oncology staff at All-Children's Hospital that year. I had hair then, so that should give you an idea of how long ago it was. You'd never know how many Christmases have come and gone by looking at the card, though. The corners haven't the slightest bend and it looks like the crayon marks were made yesterday.

Storing my most cherished holiday keepsake in an air-tight plastic sleeve, in a fire-proof safe for 364 days of the year may have something to do with the card's immaculate condition. It's my wish that after I'm gone, my family will continue the tradition of telling Sammy's story on Christmas Eve. I'd love for the card to be in presentable shape when they do.

My Christmas card from Sammy has a wavy crayon drawing of me in my white coat, the one I wore nearly every day on my rounds that year. Sammy is next to me on the bed. Santa Claus is sitting on the bed with Sammy. We're all smiling. There's a slight halo around Sammy's head, but he didn't draw it. That came when I first held the card in my hands, so many years ago, and a single tear escaped my eye and landed on Sammy's hand-drawn self-portrait. The scene is an innocent five-year-old's rendering of hope. For me, it's meant so much more. Every Christmas I adorn the mantle next to our Christmas tree with the card and tell this story about what really matters.

May it speak to you as it has to so many through the years...

Five-year-old Sammy Wilson was the first terminal case I treated in my medical career. You never forget your first, no matter how many children you may have saved since.

This isn't a sad story, though I always seem to start it off on a somber note. That's because pediatric oncology is a tough specialty. Sometimes, you lose a child whose aura pushes past your professional wall and finds its way into your heart. Sammy Wilson was one of those kids, as thoughtful and generous as any child I've ever met. He was also one of the sickest I'd treated in my career at that point. He didn't have much time left, and I couldn't give him more. I was willing, however, to do anything in my power to make the time Sammy had left special.

Sammy Wilson had an aggressive case of acute lymphoblastic leukemia—the kind that, in those days had no effective treatment. All you could hope to do was delay the inevitable by the blasting the cancer with as much chemotherapy as the child could take.

Sammy had been in an out of hospitals for most of his life. The last six months, however, had been the toughest. The chemo had taken his hair and nearly every ounce of his strength. Draining as the treatment regimen was, it wasn't enough to appease the boy's affliction. The cancer in Sammy's brittle bones just growled and kept coming, killing the child's white blood cells in droves and leaving his withering body a vulnerable open target for infectious disease.

Sammy dealt with his illness as though it were just a bump in the road on the way to the playground. Even though his sickness had kept him away from most playgrounds in his life, the boy's heart never faded. Neither did his smile.

It was December 24th and I had just gone over the latest cytogenetic analysis with Sammy's mom, when Sammy turned to her and asked the hardest question a boy can ask his mother.

Angela Wilson had done everything humanly possible for her only son. She'd taken him to every specialist on the East Coast, and spent every penny she had doing it.

To look at Sammy's mom, you would have thought she was the patient. The sleepless nights of worry had exacted a heavy toll on the woman who couldn't have been more than thirty. Her hair was thin. Her frame gaunt. Her eyes looked like they hadn't rested in years. She didn't have any delusions about what part of the journey she and Sammy had reached. Angela Wilson was a realist. Still, Sammy's question caught her off-guard.

"Mom? Will I live to see Christmas?"

Even today, I can hear Sammy's delicate voice ask his mom to predict a future she was too heartbroken to consider. Like the card he would later give me, the memory of Sammy's innocent question still makes my eyes well up with tears when I'm alone and pensive, the way a moment you were never meant to forget should.

Sammy's mom didn't tell her son the truth, not in the clinical sense anyway. Like all great answers moms provide to the really hard questions, Angela Wilson's explanation gave Sammy the comfort that there would be a tomorrow, and it would be even better than today if Sammy greeted it with love in his heart.

For the first time in my professional life, I prayed to anyone who might be listening to let Sammy Wilson live long enough to see Christmas. God didn't answer. I gave it about a 20% chance. The truth was, Sammy's bone marrow was overrun with immature lymphocytes. Any night could be his last. Leukemia doesn't care if it's Christmas Eve.

None of the patients at All-Children's Hospital are ever on the naughty list, which is why Santa Claus makes regular appearances here during the holiday season. He always makes the rounds on Christmas Eve, but Sammy was in a deep sleep when he did during this particular year. Christmas Eve is a busy time for Saint Nicholas, and the chances of getting Santa to hold his appointments to make a personal appearance for Sammy seemed a grim prognosis.

There were other kids at other hospitals, Santa assured me, who, like Sammy, wanted nothing more than to make a Christmas wish to St. Nicholas, himself. The doctor in me understood that there were other kids in need of Santa's love. There would always be others. But the thought of Sammy Wilson's last Christmas coming and going without the boy seeing Santa was too much for me to bear.

Theresa, the charge nurse on duty that night, told me about The North Pole, a talent agency that specialized in Santa Claus impersonators. Their actors, Theresa assured me, were the giants of their field, spitting reflections of the real thing, and the go-to Kris Kringles of All-Children's Hospital—largely for their ability to make special calls for time-sensitive cases like Sammy's.

We both understood that Sammy, despite his frail state, had an uncanny knack for identifying anything that fell short of the genuine truth. This went for medical explanation and iconic holiday figures. Theresa was steadfast in her support of The North Pole. Like me, she was a straight shooter when it came to treatment recommendations for tough cases. She'd been at All-Children's ten years longer than I had, which was enough for me to realize she was the expert in this delicate matter. I was convinced her prescription was the proper one, and so I made the call.

In those days, we had what were called *phone books*—tomes of newsprint and advertising that held the phone numbers of every resident and business in town. I walked my fingers through the book and found the number for The North Pole. A half-page advertisement next to the number touted the virtues of the agency, which all but assured the real Santa would be available no matter how dire the circumstances.

My heart pounded like a first-year surgeon's waiting for lab results as I dialed the number and the ring chime echoed in my ear. Four rings, then five.

Obviously they were busy. It was Christmas Eve, after all.

The line clicked on the seventh ring. There was a pause. I held my breath, then let my heart drop to my feet when I heard the hiss of the tape and the recorded voice of the answering machine (another relic from the pre-cell phone past). The North Pole was booked solid for Christmas.

I spent the next half hour desperately scanning the phone book in search of anyone who might stand in as Santa Claus and brighten Sammy Wilson's last Christmas. It was no use. My ears were continuously tortured by a cackling symphony of unrequited phone rings and campy holiday-themed answering machine messages.

Santa had left the building. All of them.

No doctor likes to admit defeat, but we all inevitably learn when it's time to accept it. Just as I had resigned to the truth that nothing more could be done, a custodian across the room opened a window. A rush of night air swept in and found the pages of the phone book, flipping the bulk of them to form a paper wave that fell on some random, useless page.

Disgusted at the prospect of failure, I snatched the phone book and was just about to slam it shut, when I saw a block-type listing whose tiny presence barely stood out from the rest on the page. My eyes focused and I took in the words: Santa's Workshop. With nothing to lose, I dialed the number and again hoped someone, anyone, would answer my prayer.

Salvation came on the fourth ring.

I can still hear the voice on the other end of the phone—so bouncy, so high-pitched and energetic, so…elf-like. Santa, the elf explained, was extremely busy this Christmas Eve. But after my pleading the details of Sammy's case, he affirmed that the Father of Christmas could indeed make time for a personal visit to see such an obviously special boy.

I waited with Sammy and his mom, who was still praying that Santa would arrive and bring joy to the boy who'd had the toughest of years. Sammy lay in his bed, asleep and at peace. The tubes that had penetrated his tiny body for as long as I could remember had lost all medical meaning to me. They'd become constant reminders of a childhood marred by undeserved hardship. I tried to imagine the visions of sugarplums dancing in Sammy's head. Then I looked at his mom, and she at me. We held our silence with the understanding that there was nothing left for us to do, except wait.

The door opened slightly and a plump, spectacled face poked through and smiled, first at Angela Wilson then at me.

"I hear there's a special boy named Sammy Wilson in here," Santa spoke in a soft voice, careful not to wake the boy he'd come to see.

Sammy's body shifted on the bed and his eyes slowly opened.

"Santa?" the boy said through a groggy voice.

"Hello, Sammy," Santa answered, sliding his round frame through the door.

"And a jolly Christmas Eve to you, Mrs. Wilson," he said as he crossed the room and shook Angela's hand. I took in Santa as though I were a boy in awe, myself. He was wearing green overalls, which seemed to me the perfect primer to his trademark red suit and cap. A coffee colored complexion peeked from behind his beard and glasses. Other than that, he looked authentic.

"And to you, Dr. Talbott." Santa extended his hand to mine and I took it, and, for reasons I still can't explain, felt rejuvenated with the power to heal.

"Shouldn't you be wearing your suit?" Sammy asked. The boy had put his finger on the ruse. I swallowed hard, while Santa stayed cool.

"Mrs. Claus is putting the finishing touches on my coat for tonight. Good thing you live where it's sunny and warm, Sammy."

"You really came all the way from the North Pole?" Sammy asked, sitting up in his bed. The boy who could spot a phony under any sedation was now convinced he was looking at the real thing.

"Santa's Workshop is working overtime tonight."

Santa gave Sammy's mom and me the slightest of winks. "The elves are finishing the last of the toys, and Rudolph is a bit under the weather. But fear not, Sammy. Mrs. Claus will make sure Santa makes the rounds to all the boys and girls this Christmas Eve. She always does."

Sammy's smile was bright enough to guide Santa's sleigh.

"Well, then young man, you and I have a great deal to talk about." Santa pulled a chair next to Sammy's bed. It was then when St. Nick noticed the cookies on the bedside table. A crayon drawing of Santa with his name written in bright red, and an arrow pointing to the plate let the world know who the treat was intended for. Sammy had insisted on leaving Santa sugar cookies with green and red icing. The boy only mildly protested when his mom procured a six-pack of Oreos and a single-serving of milk from the cafeteria.

"How did you know Oreos were my favorite?" Santa asked. Sammy looked at his mom with wide eyes of love.

"My mom said you probably would get tired of sugar cookies," Sammy said.

"Mothers do know best, Sammy," Santa replied, taking hold of an Oreo. The three of us watched as Santa unscrewed the cookie sandwich, licked the filling clean, pushed both cookies back together, dunked it into the milk, then swallowed the thing whole. His face lit with joy.

"Now then, Sammy, I have a big night ahead of me, but it can wait since you and I have a lot to discuss. I wonder if your mom and the good doctor would mind leaving us to ourselves for a few minutes."

Angela Wilson and I were all smiles as we stepped from the room. Moments after the door shut and we were in the hall, the woman who'd logged more hours that year at All-Children's Hospital than anyone on staff thanked me through tears. She gave me a hug and I told her that Santa was right. Sammy is a special boy. I stopped there, not wanting to speculate on what the future held. In that moment, the world was full of possibility.

Sammy was happy. So was his mom, and so was I.

Not more than a half hour had passed when the door opened and Santa entered, gently closing the door behind him. His eyes fell to the floor. When he pulled them up, Angela Wilson and I saw not an actor playing a role, but a man fighting back tears.

"That's quite a young man you have there, Mrs. Wilson," Santa said, pulling his glasses from his rosy face and wiping his misty eyes.

"No. Not yet," Angela said, pushing past Santa and stepping into the room. I thought of what I'd say to the mother who'd just lost her only son on Christmas Eve. It was then when I realized I hadn't heard Sammy's monitor issue the slightest warning that something was wrong.

Angela pushed to door open enough to see Sammy in bed asleep. A smile stretched across the boy's glowing face.

Santa said, "I told Sammy he could have anything in the world for Christmas, anything at all. He told me that this could be his last Christmas, and he'd given a lot of thought to what he wanted. What he wants more than anything is for all the children on this floor to get well so they can spend Christmas with their families."

Mothers are supposed to cry on the oncology floor of a children's hospital. It's expected. The unwritten rule is that doctors are expected to remain composed. Neither Angela Wilson nor I could help ourselves. Sammy Wilson likely wouldn't live through the night, but he was alive now and had just drifted to a peaceful sleep after seeing Santa Claus on Christmas Eve.

"Quite a young man," Santa said, shaking his head in amazement. "Oh, I nearly forgot. Sammy made Christmas presents." St. Nick reached into his green overalls and produced a stack of papers. He carefully selected two from the lot and handed one to me and one to Sammy's mom.

"Apparently the boy's been working on these for some time," Santa said. "There's one for every staff member on the floor."

I held the paper in my trembling hands and studied its crayoned markings. The greeting read: Dear Doktar Talbutt. There was a drawing of a stethoscope on the cover under a bright green Christmas tree. I opened the card and saw the scene that would forever bring me to tears each Christmas since. There was the now immortal, hand-drawn scene of Santa, and Sammy, and me. I couldn't take my eyes from the card, even after the tear dropped from my eye and landed on Sammy's crayon-sketched face, making him look like he'd been kissed by an angel.

I don't remember Santa saying goodbye. But I do remember standing on the roof of the hospital later that night, looking down over the lights of St. Petersburg and at the sky above. A shooting star streaked across the horizon. I tried to ignore the scientific fact that it was nothing more than the visible path of a meteoroid entering the earth's atmosphere on a one-way course with destruction. Instead, I imagined the brilliant streak was Santa's sleigh making its rounds across the world. I closed my eyes and made a wish that Sammy's wish would come true

❄ ❄ ❄ ❄ ❄

The next day's sun rose like any other. I tried to pretend like it was any morning other than Christmas as I made my way through my routine. I smiled at well-wishing colleagues in Santa hats, who bid a cheery Merry Christmas as I made my way to Sammy's room.

My palpitating heart could surely be heard without a stethoscope as I reached for Sammy's doorknob, slowly opened the door to his room and peeked my head through the threshold. The first face I saw belonged to Father Carrol, a chaplain at our hospital, who stood bedside next to Sammy's mom. Father Carrol's face was stoic, typical for him on any day—including Christmas. Angela Wilson was somber, but relieved, as though a burdening weight she'd endured for so long had at last been lifted from her shoulders. Sammy had enjoyed his last Christmas. We'd done everything to ensure he would.

I composed myself as I opened the door and walked in, ready to offer my sincerest condolences. That's when I saw Sammy. He was in his bed, sitting upright, as he played with a toy rocket ship. The smile on his face could have lit an operating room.

Sammy Wilson was alive and enjoying Christmas with his family. In my profession, miracles aren't the healthiest outcome to wish for, but once in a while, they make the world a happier place. My prayers had been answered. I was living a Christmas miracle.

Theresa the charge nurse approached with a hurried stride, a perplexing look on her face, and a stack of files in her hands.

"Doctor Talbott! Doctor Talbott!" she called, with an excited urgency. I stepped out of the room, leaving the door ajar as Theresa came to a short deceleration mere inches from me.

"Sammy's latest blood work," she said. "It's—well it's amazing." She handed me the report, so I could see with my own eyes that Sammy's white blood cell count had returned to near normal levels.

"This has to be a mistake," I said with an even tone as I glanced back through the ajar door and saw Sammy laughing in his bed and bouncing on his bottom with the vigor and vitality of boy whose endurance knew no bounds.

"It's right, doctor," Theresa confirmed with confidence. "I made the lab check three times. That's Sammy Wilson's blood analysis."

"Amazing," was all I could muster as I stared at the numbers that simply defied modern medicine. A boy who was on the verge of losing his battle with leukemia just twelve hours ago was now cancer-free.

"Doctor," Theresa said with the knowing voice of a mother who has one last present for her child to open on an already plentiful Christmas morning, "there's more."

She handed me the files of all the children on the floor. One by one I went through them, careful not to miss a single entry of data. Every child on oncology floor was not only alive and well, they had all entered remission. It's then when I picked up my head and, for the first time that Christmas morning, saw the joy on every face around me. Every nurse, every tech, every parent, and every child was smiling with life and love. Christmas had come to the oncology floor of All-Children's Hospital. Sammy Wilson's wish had come true.

My family is grown now. My children have children old enough to dream on their own. Through the years, we've always enjoyed Christmas the way it should be celebrated. Together.

Each year, when I tell the story I've just told you, someone always asks what became of Sammy. The boy who taught me to believe in miracles is himself a grown man today, with a loving family of his own. In fact, he too became a children's physician. I had the privilege of mentoring Dr. Sammy, as the kids and parents called him, before retiring myself many years ago.

And so we've come to the end of our story. I hope it's inspired you to cherish the things that matter most on Christmas. And just in case you're wondering if the Santa who visited Sammy all those years ago was real, know that a lot of kids—big and small —have asked me that question over the years.

I always took pride in being a thorough physician. For the record, I did try to call Santa's Workshop and tell Saint Nick what became of Sammy and the rest of the kids on the oncology floor at All-Children's Hospital. But when I went to the place in the phone book where the number should have been, I was surprised to discover the listing had vanished. I poured over every page of the book, with no luck. Santa's Workshop had gone the way of Sammy's cancer. It was as though it never existed.

In trying to explain the seemingly inexplicable, doctors tend to side with scientific reason as opposed to outright miraculous explanations. Maybe what happened that special Christmas Eve long ago really was a miracle, after all. I like to think so.

The truth is, even after all these years I haven't found the number for Santa's Workshop on the Internet, either.

The Closet

Lisa heard the screams and tried to make herself as small as she could. The closet she was hiding in was pitch black, not much bigger than a phone booth and smelled of bleach. But for now, it was her only refuge from the terror that reigned just beyond the darkness of her sanctuary. The sheer panic that owned Lisa in the moments leading up to now had waned, as she realized the frequency of the screams from the nearby hallways had decreased in the last few minutes. But she was still every bit as scared as when the whole thing began. She could hear her own breathing and wondered how loud it may sound to the outside world.

She hadn't heard gunshots for a while. Five minutes. Maybe more. She couldn't know for sure. The shooting began without warning and turned the school into chaos sometime during second period when she was in the library. She had left her cell phone in the reference section when it began and for the life of her couldn't remember how she got here or how long she'd been in hiding. The bell signaling the end of second period hadn't sounded, yet. Or had it? Maybe she had missed it amidst the screams. She wondered if it was all over. Perhaps somewhere in a distant corner of the school, students and teachers rejoiced and hugged each other knowing there was nothing left to fear. Fear, in all of its mental and physical anguish, was still very much alive in Lisa. She knew she couldn't get up. Fear had paralyzed her.

She had fled the library and made her way through the 700 hallway when it began. The hall was infused with kinetic horror. An aimless frenzy of kids and adults scattered in a reckless pact of mass confusion, like an anthill that had been trounced by a giant with a deadly weapon. No one knew what to do. They just ran. Lisa couldn't run. The fear had taken hold and wouldn't allow her to move any faster than a sloth in a waking dream.

As the halls thinned of people, Lisa slithered her way to the nearest exit. She turned the corner at Mr. Barlowe's room and instantly froze. At the end of the next hall stood a hooded figure dressed in black from head to toe. The figure held a rifle.

Lisa was paralyzed. In a moment the figure would see her and end what had begun with a hail of bullets she knew she'd never escape. She retreated down the 700 hallway and slipped into the janitor's closet next to Mr. Barlowe's room, expecting the figure to follow and in a moment open the door to her chamber. She kept the lights off and desperately tried to lock the closet, realizing then that she needed a key. She settled on the floor and waited. And waited. And waited.

She hunched on the floor wishing she could melt into its surface when she heard the doorknob turn. The door opened slowly, spilling a shaft of light into the closet. Lisa held her breath and tried to be still. Knowing she could never face the end with any kind of view, she closed her eyes and waited for the penetrating shot that would vanquish her fear forever. Each passing second was agonizing, a teasing killer's sadistic attempt at humor. But the end never came. Instead, the door closed.

Lisa opened her eyes to blackness. She could hear ragged breathing other than her own and knew she wasn't alone in the closet. She stayed perfectly still.

Minutes passed but felt like hours. The halls were quiet now. The two strangers in the pitch-black closet were silent, with only Lisa aware that she wasn't alone. The knowledge comforted her, though she didn't dare give herself away. The darkness seemed to slow time to a standstill. How long had it been? Maybe the gunman had given up. Maybe someone would come through the halls and announce that it was over, that everyone could come out now, as though this had all been a game of hide-and-seek. Lisa listened with hope. Then she heard two more shots.

She flinched, causing the shelf behind her to flex—a bumbling reaction Lisa wished she could take back.

"Who's there?" The voice was thin and frail with uncertainty, though clearly male. Lisa remained silent.

"Who is that? Answer me! Please!" Lisa's unseen companion uttered in a strained voice, trying to be quiet, but wanting to shout. Its timbre carried a desperation that Lisa could sense was deeper than her own.

"I'm here," whispered Lisa, trying to sound warm and reassuring. "I'm sitting on the floor behind you."

"Who are you?"

"It's Lisa Capehart. I'm a sophomore."

"The door won't lock."

"I know," said Lisa. "It only locks with a key."

"How long have you been here?" The voice was still gripped with fear.

"I've been here the whole time," said Lisa, "since the shooting began."

"Who did it? Who did the shooting?"

"I don't know. I saw someone, but I don't know who."

"Who? Who did you see?" His level of panic was rising.

"Who are *you?*" Lisa thought familiarity might make them both feel better in the darkness. Yet her question was met with silence.

"I'm Lisa Capehart," repeated Lisa, this time with an intense focus on being calm. "I'm a sophomore. Who are you?"

"Ricky. Ricky Sampson. I'm a ... I'm a junior."

"You're a free safety on the football team, Ricky. You had three interceptions last year and were second team all-conference."

Ricky's panic turned to genuine shock. "How'd you know that?"

"I'm on the yearbook staff," said Lisa. "I was looking over this year's stats when..." She trailed off. "When all this began."

There was silence for a moment.

"I don't know you," Ricky said.

"It's OK. You know me now." Lisa let out a sigh that calmed her and seemed to ease Ricky, if only for a moment.

"I'm gonna hit the lights," he said.

"No!" Lisa managed to keep her voice at a low whisper. "They can see that from the hall. Leave it off."

Ricky complied, but Lisa could now feel his physical uneasiness hang between them, creating an even more desolate mood that neither of them wanted to acknowledge.

"Lisa?" Ricky sounded calmer, though Lisa wondered if the darkness helped their situation or made it more uncertain. "Is there room on the floor?" Ricky sat before she could answer, and Lisa could sense his presence next to her. He was still a stranger, but she felt safer knowing he was now by her side.

"I saw someone," said Ricky in a struggling low voice. "I saw someone … get shot." Lisa listened, not wanting to hear the rest, but knowing she had to for Ricky's sake. "It was Jeremy Skoelnick. I was running through the 900 hall. I turned into the 700 hallway, and he was there. Standing in the hall. He looked at me. Like he was scared. And then it was like his chest exploded. But he just looked at me. Even when he was on the floor, he looked at me. He reached his hand up to me. And I ran. I ran and I hid in here."

Ricky was in tears. Lisa could tell. She had known Jeremy Skoelnick since the fourth grade, though they weren't friends these days. They weren't anything now. Jeremy was dead. His mother didn't know it yet, but Lisa did. His lifeless body was probably still in the 700 hallway, just outside the closet she and Ricky shared. Jeremy Skoelnick. He was always smart. Good with computers, and funny. Lisa had Geometry with him in the ninth grade. He understood the proofs and theorems that had baffled her for most of the semester. He was smart.

"Did you know him?" Lisa quietly asked.

"I made fun of him last week," Ricky fought back more tears. "I don't even know why. Something he was wearing, maybe. He didn't say anything. He just looked at me." Ricky couldn't fight the tears anymore. He cried and Lisa listened.

"I can't get his face out of my mind. He just looked at me." Ricky's whimpers grew louder. Lisa knew she had to do something or they'd both be found.

"Ricky, listen to me." Lisa's voice was steady. "I knew Jeremy. We talked yesterday. He wasn't hurt by you or what you said. He didn't have any hard feelings." It was a lie, but it made Ricky feel better.

"I'm sorry," Ricky's sobs regressed to a sniffle. "I'm so sorry."

"Ricky," Lisa tried to sound as sincere as she could, "I know you're sorry, but we have to be quiet. We just have to be quiet and stay here until it's all over."

They leaned into each other in silence. The halls were now ghostly quiet and Lisa tried to occupy her racing mind by replaying the images from when it all began. It was second period and she was in Yearbook. Tuesdays were research days; and on this morning Lisa was in the library at one of the computers, looking at football stats that she might use in the layout for the upcoming annual. Everything seemed so normal. The library was quiet, just as it had been on every Tuesday of the year thus far. Then she saw Jenn Rogers run past her table like a flash. Then Lisa fell back in her chair like something had kicked her. Then she was up and in the hallway, moving against the grain of the panicking student body. Then she was staring at the figure. Then she was lying on the floor in the closet. She started to shiver.

"Are you OK?" Ricky asked.

"I'm cold," said Lisa. Ricky tried to put his arm around her. It was an instinctive reaction, an attempt at comforting her more than anything else. Lisa cringed at the touch, prompting Ricky to quickly withdraw his arm.

"I'm sorry," Ricky blurted, "I just — "

"It's OK. It's not you."

"What the hell is this?" Ricky said. "Why are you all wet?"

"I'm not wet."

"Wait a minute." Ricky sprang to his feet and hit the light switch, which harshly illuminated the closet in a flickering instant, causing Lisa to squirm. Ricky looked at his hands. They were covered in blood.

"What the...?" He looked at Lisa on the floor below. She writhed in a pool of her own blood, her clothes stained red. "Jesus, you were shot?"

"I'm OK. Turn off the light."

"The hell you are. We can't stay here. We've got to get you to a doctor."

"No! We have to stay here."

"Lisa, you've been shot. I don't know how bad, but you've been shot. And it's not gonna get any better if we stay here. We've got to get you out."

"I can't," Lisa's voice trembled as tears rolled down her face. "I can't walk," she whimpered in a barely audible rasp. "I can't walk."

Ricky dropped back to the floor and put his arm around Lisa, who buried her face in Ricky's chest and sobbed. Ricky held her until her heaving gasps slowed down.

"Lisa, listen to me." Ricky was calm as he spoke, "There's a first-aid kit in Mr. Barlowe's classroom."

"No."

"It's just at the end of the hall."

"No."

"I'll only be gone a minute."

"Don't leave me."

"I'll only be gone a minute. Then I can help you."

"Please, don't leave me." Lisa held him tight, refusing to let go. Ricky stood and pulled away until Lisa had no choice but to give up her grip.

"I'll only be gone a minute. You can time me." Lisa imagined he smiled, aware she would have no way to know for sure how long he would be gone.

"Ricky—," her voice trailed off. Ricky slowly turned the knob and cracked the door open enough to assess the hall. He could see Jeremy Skoelnick's body between the closet and Mr. Barlowe's room, and knew he'd have to look in Jeremy's eyes again. He glanced back at Lisa and saw she had slumped to the floor. Her prone body was fading, and Ricky couldn't help but think she didn't have much time left.

"I'll be back in a minute," he said. Lisa summoned every ounce of strength she had to impart one final request before Ricky ventured into the unknown to save her life.

"Turn the light off, please."

Ricky took Lisa in and hated himself for thinking this could be the last time her ever saw her. Then he turned off the lights. She didn't have long, Ricky thought as he stepped out to the hall and closed the door behind him, leaving Lisa guarded only by the hauntingly familiar company of darkness.

She had no way to know for sure how long Ricky would be gone, so she started to count. First in her head, then continuing aloud. "…eleven, twelve, thirteen, fourteen … thirty-four, thirty-five … seventy-nine, eighty, eighty-one … one hundred eighteen, one hundred nineteen…" Two minutes had passed. Then she heard a gunshot.

The shot was close. Closer than it had been before. Lisa wanted to run to Ricky. She wanted to flee from the closet that had suddenly started to feel like a coffin. She tried to get to her feet and rise to the door, but she couldn't stand. She couldn't move. She was bound to the floor and resigned to accept whatever fate lurked beyond the closet. She closed her eyes.

Minutes passed. Maybe hours. Lisa had tried to continue counting, but drifted in and out of consciousness. She opened her eyes as she heard the doorknob turn and was blinded by the flood of light that spilled into the closet. Lisa looked up and saw the figure in black. The silhouette moved toward her. She closed her eyes and waited for the end, hoping it would be quick and without the pain she wondered if she could even feel anymore.

She didn't see her life pass before her eyes as she thought she might. Instead she saw her ninth-grade Geometry class. She saw a half-worked proof on the board next to what she imagined were congruent triangles. She looked to her left and saw Jeremy Skoelnick, who seemed to understand. He was always smart. It would be over soon. She'd come to accept her fate and had finally evolved beyond the paralyzing grip her fear had held over her. She felt hands on her body as she rolled onto her back. Then she heard Ricky's voice.

"Lisa! Lisa!" Ricky was alive with excitement. Lisa opened her eyes and saw him. She tried to get up and felt herself restrained.

"It's OK, Miss Capehart." This from a broad-shouldered man Lisa took to be someone who could help. "We're going to take care of you. Just try and stay down. We're going to help you."

"It's over, Lisa. It's all over," Ricky said as he knelt by Lisa's side. She looked at him as the paramedic slid an oxygen mask over her mouth and instructed her to breathe slowly.

"I told you I'd be back," Ricky said with an easy smile that warmed Lisa. She felt her body lift to the heavens, only to be lowered and then secured onto a gurney.

She wanted to be clever and say to Ricky with a movie star's sarcastic grace, "Took you long enough!" But she couldn't muster the strength, so instead she simply smiled and reached for Ricky's hand.

"You're going to be OK," Ricky said with a tear in his eye that told Lisa he meant it. She wanted to say, "Thanks to you," but would settle for, "I know." When neither would come from her mouth, she squeezed Ricky's hand, looked him in the eyes and smiled.

She knew, and so did he.

Nebraska Avenue

The terminal at Tampa's Union Station was hardly the grand affair Ellie's teenage mind had conjured during the previous four hours aboard a cramped Amtrak. There was no sailor in white sparking up a cigarette after plopping down a well-travelled duffel bag. No elegant dame in a flapper skirt leaning into the strong arms of a handsome man in a fedora. No railroad officer in a blue uniform urging a lovesick soldier to board the departing train. The only man in uniform Ellie spotted had to be one of Tampa's finest, judging from the badge on the chest and the gun on the hip of the muscle-bound brute who crossed the room and escorted a bearded man with leathery skin and dirty clothes to the door after he'd fallen to a prone position on one of the benches. Sleeping, Ellie deduced, was forbidden in Union Station if you looked a certain way.

Ellie put a cigarette between her lips. But before she could strike her lighter, an angry voice reverberated from behind the ticket counter. Her eyes met the bellower, who emphatically pointed to a sign that indicated smoking wasn't allowed in Union Station, either. With no hint of apology, she pocketed her lighter and left the cigarette dangling from her lips as she slowly crossed the floor, her heels tapping a rhythmic cadence against the tile. Thus far, Tampa wasn't living up to its reputation, at least not the one Ellie had imagined.

Her month-long, late-night Internet research binge revealed that Tampa was the Cigar City and birthplace of the lap dance, where gangsters once reigned like drunken dinosaurs fighting for supremacy over land that would someday house a strip mall. Sin City, Ellie had decided, wasn't in Las Vegas. Even if it were, she didn't have a cousin living there as she did in Tampa so the point was moot. This was where her summer adventure would occur. Rent-free accommodations had an undeniable appeal. And given Ellie's budget, free was fast becoming her favorite number.

Wikipedia hadn't mentioned a word about the humidity that slugged Ellie across the face the moment she stepped from the terminal to the outside world. An indigo haze followed the retiring sun over the horizon as lights winked across the downtown skyline. Ellie glanced at her watch out of habit even though she knew it was still on back-home time. After a quick calculation of the time change, she knew her cousin was late. Typical. She hadn't seen Klause since she was 10 years old, but knew even then he was flake. Apparently not much had changed.

Her cell phone was dead, having run out of charge sometime while she was in-flight. Even if she could call Klause — and the thought of using a Union Station pay phone did present a certain nostalgic charm — her lay-about slacker of a cousin wouldn't answer. She'd wait for him, but not for long.

Ellie leaned against a light pole and lit another cigarette, striking a pose and artfully exhaling smoke as though she had an audience. When her cig was almost to the filter she stamped it out and waited a minute before lighting the next one. Chain-smoking held no dignity, she had come to reason, recalling the scores of pot-bellied men back home who gave the practice anything but a glamorous standing.

Three smokes later with no sign of her cousin, Ellie decided she'd had enough. Suddenly her father's insistence to ship her luggage seemed like a clairvoyant stroke of genius, since her imminent trek as a pedestrian would certainly be more urban chic without the burden of dragging a suitcase.

Cities were meant to be explored on foot. Ellie couldn't recall the origin of the phrase, but it played in her mind like a mantra as she crossed the parking lot and headed north on Nebraska Avenue toward a place called Sulphur Springs, where her cheese-brained cousin dwelled. She couldn't say for sure how much ground she'd have to cover, but the journey promised the kind of adventure Ellie knew the City of Tampa wouldn't include in its tourist brochures, which made it all the more appealing. She could imagine the veins in her father's neck pounding through his skin at the thought of his only daughter traversing such an urban landscape at the onset of night. Her parents were against the trip from the beginning, but which of Ellie's decisions *weren't* the killjoys against these days? They threatened to disown her when she dyed her hair a neon shade of lollipop-pink, and were a phone call away from summoning a priest to perform an exorcism when she pierced her nose. When they saw Ellie's tongue had fallen prey to her recently acquired piercing fetish, her father had turned to bribery and offered to pay for a summer frolic. Maybe it was a parent's last-ditch effort to send his only daughter on an oats-sowing excursion before he spontaneously combusted. Good thing the old man didn't have a clue about the tattoo she'd permanently decorated her back and nether region with sometime during the wine-sloshed night before she hopped a plane and then a train bound for Tampa. That would have given the old man a coronary. Eventually, it may still.

She was far from home now, far from the overbearing scrutiny of her parents. She was free. America the beautiful was built on freedom and the desire to live without the pains of oppression, was it not? God bless America, Ellie thought as she turned away from the crashing waves of interstate noise and began her trek up the sidewalk along Nebraska Avenue, Cigar City's most notorious thoroughfare.

With her cell phone out of commission, traveling music would be up to Ellie's imagination. She mentally ran through all her playlists searching for the appropriate tune to set the mood.

As she crossed the tracks just before a street named Cass, the bass-driven rattle of an approaching vehicle interjected its own musical suggestion. Ellie knew what kind of buildings lay ahead. Here in Tampa they'd be called projects. Back home, they wouldn't be spoken of. Hip-hop, too, was something of a de facto outlaw where she was from, yet the indiscernible lyrics emitting from the approaching vehicle brought a smile to Ellie's face. She knew it was a well-practiced art in a place like Tampa to turn an automobile into a subwoofer-on-wheels that blasted its volume from street to street for all to hear, another ritual that was frowned upon back home.

The sounds drew closer. Closer. Still closer, until Ellie had to turn to see what approached her. Instinctive reaction forced her to jump from the sidewalk like an off-balanced bullfighter to make way for the source of the music. It was then Ellie realized that the sounds she had heard came not from a car roving the urban landscape, but from an oversized tricycle. Mounted between its rear wheels was a mammoth speaker that pulsed like a throbbing heart with each clattering beat. The rider, a shirtless man with rippling dark skin and a head of frizzled black hair, didn't look back at Ellie as he crossed Cass Street and headed east toward the projects. Innovation, Ellie thought, as she reestablished her path on the sidewalk. Wikipedia hadn't mentioned that about Tampa, either.

She didn't see the elderly man sitting under the overpass, at least not right away. But she could hear the sound of his harmonica lofting its melody into the rafters of the highway barrier above, where it danced among the passing cars as though the sounds were trading fours in a heated jazz improvisation. As Ellie advanced beneath the overpass, she saw a man in dark sunglasses seated against one of the mighty pillars with his back to Nebraska Avenue and his heart focused on creating soulful sounds Ellie had only ever heard in old movies.

This was a street performer whose efforts were certainly worthy of some spare change, yet Ellie knew she had none. She didn't have any money save for a fistful of traveler's checks her father had demanded she attain before her departure. She felt remiss that she couldn't show her appreciation to the artist by contributing to his offering pot, as she knew was the native custom, but soon realized the man had no pot to speak of. Perhaps, she reasoned, his motives were altruistic and he simply wanted to fill the Tampa night with sounds the city had long forgotten. A romantic gesture Ellie silently commended as she walked past the man, who paid her absolutely no attention as he continued to blow his mouth harp with a rigorous passion that seemed to intensify as she drew near. He was blind, which didn't seem fair given that the man was more than holding up his end of the relationship with the street. He would never see the smiles his music elicited from passersby who enjoyed his melodies for free.

Ellie opted not to look back as she continued north, crossing beneath the other side of the overpass and stepping out of its amplified theatre. As she walked north, she could still hear the sounds. And as they grew more faint, Ellie wondered why her father could ever object to her coming to such a cultured place.

The sounds of the harmonica waltzed in Ellie's head for the next hour or so, oscillating between harmony and discord against the visuals of the Tampa night. They seemed to perfectly fit the commencement of a church ceremony as a flood of believers with skin as dark as the night congregated around a worn brick building whose urban holiness could use a makeover. Most of the crowd didn't notice Ellie, but those who did seemed eager to break eye contact. A few of them merely shook their heads.

Upon viewing the flashing lights of a police cruiser in an abandoned lot several blocks later, Ellie tried to purge the harmonica's soulful tune from her mind, believing that the score was inappropriate for the present scene. Then she saw the handcuffs forcibly slapped on a man with utter defeat in his eyes, his freedom taken by a light-skinned officer who seemed to be enjoying himself a bit more than the situation warranted. In that moment, Ellie identified with the soon-to-be-incarcerated captive. What had he done to deserve such a punishment? Ellie knew the frustration of being misunderstood by the world and felt a tinge of guilt over the fact that she was free. After the man was forcefully pushed into the back of the police car, he locked eyes with Ellie through the bulletproof window, his hardened glare saying *You're nothing like me. Remember that.*

As Ellie continued north along the avenue, historic architecture gave way to a seedy run of motels and liquor stores. The new scenery brought with it a predictable change in the local inhabitants, who seemed perfectly at home amid the gritty urban landscape. The night had grown more humid and the cast of Nebraska Avenue moved about the stage with a collective intoxication that Ellie found charming.

Half a block later, Ellie could sense a car slowing along the road just behind her, as though the vehicle had singled her out for an impromptu binge of roadside stalking. She peeked over her left shoulder and saw what she instantly recognized to be a sports car, perfectly equipped for an American midlife crisis. Nothing too flashy or exotic, but enough contour and horsepower that Ellie suspected it was compensating for some lacking aspect of the owner's life. She could see this particular owner waving at her through the windshield. When the car pulled alongside Ellie, she peered through the passenger window to find a clean-cut man in his thirties, a banker maybe, or even a doctor. The driver motioned for her to come closer and Ellie obliged, lighting a cigarette and taking slow, confident strides toward the car. Her thin black skirt worked its magic against her long teenage legs as she approached the window. The man's eyes widened as Ellie leaned into the vehicle. She blew a pall of smoke into the car, a gesture that seemed to captivate the driver, who spoke in short, nervous bursts that Ellie couldn't understand, not that she really tried. Beads of sweat lined the man's forehead as he reached inside his suit jacket and pulled out a wallet, prompting Ellie to think he might ask her to make change. Their exchange was interrupted by a police car that charged past them and rocketed north on Nebraska with its lights flashing and sirens blazing a pounding alarm, buzzing the duo with a force of air. By the time Ellie returned her eyes to the driver, he had tucked his wallet back in his jacket and had his car in gear. She stepped back as he pulled away from the curb and quickly made a three-point turn, heading in the opposite direction of whatever had attracted the pursuing police cruiser.

She turned back to the sidewalk to find a rail-thin woman with molasses colored skin wearing a tight purple dress and platform heels Ellie knew she herself couldn't walk more than a few feet in without risking a broken ankle. This woman, who must have been at least six feet tall, spoke in a deep, raspy voice Ellie couldn't understand despite its musical inflection. When the heel-walker realized words were failing, she resorted to charades and pantomimed the act of smoking a cigarette, then pointed at Ellie's hip and locked eyes with her. This was the part where Ellie was supposed to give the stranger a smoke. She complied, and the stranger placed the cig between her lips like a man and sparked it like a construction worker.

While Ellie thought the two might share a moment together, the woman looked at her with hard eyes that said,

You're not welcome here then silently added *bitch* as she waved her gaunt hand as though she were trying to shoo a fly. Ellie caught the drift and headed north without so much as a word or a glance back.

The advancing hour did little to quell the smothering heat. Judging by the intoxication levels displayed by the patrons of a concrete building Ellie took to be one of the all-nude establishments that Tampa was known for, she could tell the evening's festivities were well underway. The locals let her pass without much fanfare, which, given the attention she'd attracted thus far, surprised Ellie. Any misogynistic sentiments along this stretch of Nebraska appeared to have taken a backseat to loud and heated man-to-man exchanges Ellie didn't try to decipher. She was content to press on as the clouds debated whether to hose Nebraska Avenue down with a nocturnal shower.

She doubled her pace when the first clap of thunder smacked the sky like a gong laced with shards of glass and dashed through the pouring rain until she reached the shelter of a bus stop just shy of an avenue called Lake. Fitting, given her now-saturated state.

As she ran her fingers through her hair and wrung out any lingering rainwater, Ellie noticed she wasn't alone in the bus stop. An elderly man with a full head of white, curly hair—save for a fist-sized bald patch at the crown—sat on the bench facing Nebraska Avenue. He was waiting for something. Not a bus, she reasoned. She doubted even a city like Tampa provided its denizens with public transportation at this late hour. This man looked like he would know that. No, something else called him. His slouching posture and quiet gaze suggested a broken soul waiting on a friend who fudged the date and thought he meant *next* Tuesday. Maybe, Ellie thought, the two had something in common, as she had come to believe her vacant-minded cousin had botched his own pickup date and was probably on his second round of nachos and ranch dip by now.

Perhaps it was simply youth the man missed. Clearly, she was on the opposite end of life's pendulum, closer to the beginning than the end. Whatever road lay ahead for Ellie was one she had plenty of time to explore. Nothing is permanent to a teenager. She could alter her route at any time if she felt like changing direction. Youth afforded such luxuries, which is why she could never fathom her parents becoming so critically flabbergasted at every bold move she decided to make. Why roam the paved and predictable path like everyone else, especially if it led anywhere near the dull apathy of people like her short-sighted parents? Ellie's ultimate goal this summer was to take the first steps in seizing ownership of her life. She looked forward to the long road ahead, relishing her freedom of choice, aware that time only flowed one way. Forward. There would eventually come a day when she would look back on her choices, when youth itself would be a memory. Her legs would fatten. Her breasts would sag. Someday, all she would have of her blooming years would be the memories she created today. Maybe thoughts of yesteryear were the company the man in the bus shelter sought. When he cleared a newspaper off the bench space beside him and gently smiled at Ellie, she knew he was politely asking for a friend. Ellie could be that. It was raining, after all.

She eased herself onto the bench as the rain intensified from a calm shower to a relentless pounding. Any attempt at conversation with her new friend would be futile given the ambient noise of the rainfall, so the two remained taciturn and stared at Nebraska Avenue, watching the slanting sheets of water descend from the heavens and assault the street Ellie had chosen as the entry point for her summer adventure in Tampa.

Steam rose from the ground like ghostly spirits out for a summer stroll, and Ellie couldn't help but acknowledge the utter lack of tension between her and the stranger. His aura was void of any threatening presence. He simply stared out at the rain.

Her thoughts returned to the speculation of what was promenading in the stranger's mind. She began inventing a narrative to satisfy her curiosity. He was a dancer in his youth, a good one who had his elbow-brush with fame. He needed only to rise to his toes and hold the position just long enough to grasp it. Then came the girl. She was beautiful, of course. But there was something more in the sparks that flew between them when the two locked eyes for the very first time while waiting for a trolley at this very stop. It was love, a passion so divine he would give up his selfish ambitions and marry the girl in a small ceremony attended only by the closest of friends and dearest of loved ones.

The couple made the kind of plans lovers do when life is new and open with the thrill of possibility, when the number of tomorrows far exceeds the count of yesterdays. The world, small and perfect, was theirs.

Then came the war. To Ellie, it was a conflict she would only know of from a history book. But to this man, it was the hell that took him away from his beloved. There was a defined enemy, as American wars tend to have, but this man's only true foe was time. Every moment he spent away from his love was one in which he fell closer to death by way of a broken heart.

The war finally ended and the soldier returned home, where he started a family—a large one with seven kids, who grew up happy and had kids of their own. The man watched it all through the same eyes that now stared out at Nebraska Avenue. The same eyes that gazed upon his beloved every day and night in the hospital as she withered down a dying path, afflicted with a disease the doctors were helpless to reverse. Decades of vibrant life had passed since the war, yet the man now found himself again in a battle against time. Life's pendulum had swung the other way, and he found himself pleading with the same God he had so often asked to speed up the next sunrise during the war. Now he humbly begged to extend what little time he had left with the woman who made his world.

Time, Ellie knew as she wiped a tear from her eye, would never stop. The best we can hope for is a rainstorm heavy enough to slow us down long enough to appreciate it all.

The rain eventually subsided, prompting Ellie to rise and continue her journey. Before she embarked down the freshly cleansed avenue, she looked at the stranger who still held his gaze on Nebraska. She blew him a kiss before taking her leave from the shelter. She never looked back as she walked away, but in the coda to her imagined narrative, she could see the stranger as he maintained his vigil at the bus stop that had changed his life. He was smiling.

Ellie crossed from Nebraska's east bank to its west at a street called Chelsea, and aimed her stride toward the glow of festive lights that adorned an auto service station, which boasted a pile of tires stacked so haphazardly high they must have been put there on purpose. Whatever party had taken place was over, and now all that remained—save for the cups and beer bottles strewn about the grounds—were two men seated on smaller tire stacks listening to music Ellie knew to be Latin in origin. Salsa, or was it Samba? One of the men, a portly soul who had sweated through his tuxedo hours ago, started to sing in a language Ellie recognized as Spanish. It was a language she didn't understand, yet she somehow grasped the meaning through the man's passionate tone and the universal language of music. She couldn't help but find the groove inherent in the song and move her body accordingly.

The second man stood and approached Ellie with a matador's purpose in his eyes and a caballero's grace in his stride. Men didn't come in this variety where Ellie was from, tall and lean with olive skin that glowed and rippled in all the right places. He extended his hand to her like a gentleman from a more civilized generation, and in a deep and level voice said, "¿Me concedes éste baile?"

Ellie didn't understand the words, yet took his hand in hers upon catching a glimpse of the man's smile as the glint of the lights sparkled in his captivating eyes. He pulled her towards him in a way that made Ellie spin and land with perfect form into his body, where she stayed for an instant, then returned to her starting position when the man extended both of his arms and eased her into a pose in sync with the beat. He wanted to dance, and clearly this was a man who knew how to get what he wanted.

The lead was his and the man deftly moved both of their bodies over the asphalt dance floor as though it were center stage at the most majestic ballroom Ellie could imagine. Her heart began to flutter as he locked his eyes on hers and moved his hips with such force Ellie couldn't help but follow and wonder what other powers he may possess off the dance floor. He spun her into him and then away in a tantalizing rhythm that made her blood rush, never wavering in his lustful gaze or commanding posture. The music reached a crescendo, and the man pulled Ellie toward him for the finale, lifting her from the street to the heavens and landing her back to earth in a bent drop Ellie hoped would end in a moonlit kiss. She peered through her lashes to find his eyes locked on hers. *This is the moment,* she thought. The perfect culmination of a flawless routine. She closed her eyes gently, so as not to seem desperate or overly eager, and waited to receive his soft lips on hers. The anticipation only heightened her surging energy, a tactical move made by a man who understood the nature of timing and the inherent romance involved in marrying action with moment. Another beat passed, then Ellie felt a pull and suddenly she was on her feet.

She opened her eyes as the man took a stately half-step away from her. He looked deep into her soul and smiled graciously, bowing as he still held her hands in his.

"Gracias," she said softly, cursing herself for not learning more Spanish in school.

"El placer era mía," the man returned. Just then, Ellie's alluring dance partner was playfully attacked by two young children. Each grabbed one of his legs like they were expecting a ride. "Papa!" they shouted in unison as the man bent to their level, scooped them up into his arms and lovingly spoke to them in his native tongue. All the while he backed his way toward a woman who stood in a doorway, backlit by a light from within that outlined her curvy silhouette. When all four were together, Ellie could see that this was a family whose love for one another would never wane, no matter what challenges life may instigate. Ellie turned and strode north on Nebraska Avenue, deciding it was better to not look back, a policy she'd successfully maintained thus far on her trip. But she couldn't help herself. And as she glanced over her shoulder, she saw the man's gorgeous eyes one final time as he waved to Ellie in a way that seemed to wish her luck on the journey ahead. Then he placed his hand on his wife's swollen belly that would bring another child within a month. Love, Ellie thought. There was no mistaking it.

It was well after midnight when Ellie crossed the Hillsborough River and veered off Nebraska Avenue at an old theater called The Springs. Her cousin's home was down a street named Sitka, which Ellie could instantly discern was void of the culture and charm of Nebraska Avenue. Dew clung to the canopied foliage. It would be morning soon, and Ellie replayed the events of the night's journey in her mind, bringing each of Nebraska Avenue's individual characters to life for a final bow before she reached her destination. The oversized-tricycle rider, who turned his three wheels into a rolling subwoofer. The blind harmonica player, who transformed an under-the-bridge thoroughfare into a soulful music haven. The churchgoers, who looked at Ellie as if she were a sinner-in-training. The handcuffed dark man in the police car, who warned her with his eyes not to tempt fate. The tall woman in the tight purple dress, who guarded her territory like a mother lioness. The stranger she imagined had lost his beloved, waiting and hoping for one last glimpse of her at a bus stop before rejoining her in Heaven. The dancer. That wonderful dancer with whom Ellie fell foolishly in love, even if only for a dreamlike moment filled with passion and movement.

Ellie had come to Tampa in search of memories she could capture for her life's vault. She sought both experiences and emotions that would endure and could never be commandeered by her parents, who suddenly seemed like less of an overbearing nuisance and more like caring souls whose naivety would forever hinder the job Ellie knew they were sworn to do. She would write them a letter tomorrow, a note that would omit the gritty details in telling them she'd arrived in Tampa unscathed. She'd still keep her tattoo a secret, but she'd be sure to mention to her parents that she loved them. She'd write it in a way that let both of them know she meant it.

The overflowing ashtrays and crushed beer cans that cluttered Klause's front porch foreshadowed the dinginess that awaited on the apartment's interior. Ellie's pounded the weathered front door with her open palm. Her battering maintained a steady cadence. She knew her cousin would certainly be up at this hour, whatever it was, yet might not move from the comforts of the couch unless she kept up a constant thumping that was persistent enough in its annoyance to inspire action. About the time her palm was getting sore, the door opened and Klause emerged in a mustard-stained tank top that stretched with the hundred or so pounds he had put on since last she saw him.

"Pusbrolis?" he wondered aloud in his native Lithuanian tongue. "Jūsų traukinys buvo šiandien?"

Of course he'd mixed up the date of her arrival and admitted as much, yet Ellie couldn't help but smile knowing the serendipitous reward her cousin's incompetence had provided.

"Jūs vaikščiojo visą kelią čia?" he asked. Ellie nodded to acknowledge Klause's suspicion that she had, in fact, walked all the way from the train station to his home, then placed a cigarette between her lips.

"Jūs neturėtumėte padarei, kad pusbrolis. Tai bloga kaimynystė," he said with plausible concern in his tone.

Ellie paused for a moment to consider her cousin's assessment that she had put herself at risk by walking alone in such a dangerous neighborhood. Then she casually uttered, "Aš ne pastebėjau." Her calm reply indicated that she hadn't noticed any of the perils that her conservative cousin lamented. She lit her cigarette and crossed the threshold into the home that smelled as it looked. Along the way, Ellie decided that she would add learning English to her list of things to do on her summer adventure in Tampa. As she took another drag of her smoke and recalled the strong hands of the dancer, she thought learning Spanish might not be such a bad idea, either.

About the stories

Midnight Blues

Tim and Audrey's barbecue jams were always on a Sunday. As hosts, they figured since most of their friends worked the next day, the party would never get too out-of-hand if it was on a Sunday. That was the theory, anyway.

It was a beer-soaked Sunday in 2003 maybe 2004, long enough ago no one would crucify me if I buried it in the part of the brain that keeps a sloppy archive of the day-drunk shenanigans that happened back then.

Something special took place that day, though few know about it. A group of musicians no one has ever heard of made a recording, a spectacular recording that would come to be called "Let Me Hold You."

I was in the homemade studio when it happened, and I've played the ensuing recording a thousand times since then, though I'm sure I'm the only one who still listens to it. Hell, I may be the person alive who still has a working copy.

Glad I do. It would become the inspiration and central plot device for a story that took me more than ten years to write.

The story about "Let Me Hold You" in "Midnight Blues" is made up. What comes next is the truth.

Gainesville, Florida is a music town. People will try to tell you that it's a college town or a football town, but they're only identifying possessives that every small city with a state university can claim.

Since the late 1960s, when a little band called The Epics with a little singer named Tom Petty played everywhere from house parties to student unions to the infamous and now defunct Dub's Lounge, Gainesville has had a thriving music scene.

No one was more integral to keeping that scene alive from 1996 to 2008 than Tim Reynolds.

When journalists write about great music scenes in America, they tend to forget about guys like Tim. They remember and give due credit to the bands, the fans, the venues, the record shops, the label owners, the fanzines, and even the photographers and drug dealers. But they often skip over the Tims, and I'll bet every great music scene that's ever blossomed in America—from Athens to Seattle—had one just like him.

Tim was the mainstay of Tim & Terry's Music and More, a boutique music store just off University Avenue across from the University of Florida's campus. It didn't have the widest selection of inventory (though Tim had a knack for finding and selling some choice pieces over the years, including a 1960s four-piece Slingerland drum set purchased by yours truly). The place didn't always have the best deals in town, though affordable drum sticks and guitar strings kept the working class pickers and bangers coming through. It was also music store you could smoke in during a decade when smokers were being rounded up, shot in the streets, and dumped in mass graves.

The place had heart and character.

Tim & Terry's was *the* go-to music store for the kids in the scene because the place had Tim, and if you needed your guitar or amp fixed in a pinch, Tim was your savior.

Over the years, Tim kept many an indie band on the stage with his emergency repairs and pay-me-when-you-can policies. Though he was a completely self-taught technician, he understood the inner workings of an electric guitar the way a surgeon understands human anatomy.

You don't need a license to diagnose and fix an ax or an amp in time for its owner to make a local gig, you just need heart and ingenuity. Tim had plenty of both. Ask any band who was on the scene back then, chances are they've got a story about how Tim saved their ass.

He was the unsung hero of the Gainesville scene.

Tim married Audrey in the late 90s. They lived in a house off Highway 441 (yeah, they could hear the cars roll by) with an offset garage. To a musical tinker like Tim, an offset garage isn't a place for lawnmowers and paint supplies. It's a home studio. That's what Tim built about the same time the Twin Towers fell.

His closest friends helped him with the construction. When it was done, Tim christened the studio with a name that reflected how it came to be and who is was for. He called it *The Toad House*.

As studios go, The Toad House wasn't glamorous. It had all the basics and a little extra where it mattered: The recording that would later be named "Let Me Hold You" was captured on analog equipment (like Mamie Rogers, Tim was dragged into the 21st-century kicking and smoking).

The live room in The Toad House was a tight space, but it had good sight lines so the musicians could keep eye contact with each other (a must as any studio rat will tell you). And you could smoke. You were encouraged to smoke. On most days the air in the Toad House was thick with palls of haze like a bohemian bar in post-war Europe. For smokers it was The Alamo. Last one alive topple over the smoldering ashtray and burn the place to the ground.

Tim and Audrey's Sunday barbecue jams were a glowing light that drew a range of musical bugs. Young gunslingers and old pros alike descended on that little house in Northwest Gainesville because it was where the action was.

Like a basketball court in an inner city, all you had to do was gather a few players, call "next," and the Toad House was yours for a few improvised jams. It was the thing to do in between beers and the next round of grilled oysters. Everyone played. Everyone rocked.

That's exactly how "Let Me Hold You" was recorded one Sunday afternoon.

In "Midnight Blue," Mamie confesses that the players on obscure blues recordings aren't always known. In the case of "Let Me Hold You" (the real version), I know who played the notes because I was there.

It was late in the afternoon. Crushed cans of beer were strewn about the studio, many of them overflowing with grimy cigarette butts and sloshy ash. Much of the party had staggered home, but George Covington III was still on the drums. Tim Reynolds was on the bass. His brother, Kevin, on a guitar, and Audrey Reynolds stepped into the studio for the first time of the day.

The quartet didn't speak. They just played. What they played is described as well as I can do it in "Midnight Blue." What I can add about witnessing the live performance is the truth that when Audrey belted out her sustained vibrato, The Toad House shook like it was inside a church bell.

The sound entranced me the way live music can when the boundary between listener and performer is shattered by emotion and proximity. I swore I'd been transported to another time when music wasn't made on a computer with pitch-correcting software but in a smokey room like this one, where musicians played with their souls laid bare and rolling analog tape captured it all.

It was a moment I'll never forget. I remember praying that someone less inebriated than I had the sense to push record and roll the tape so this performance—this musical instance I knew could never be recreated—was forever preserved.

It was.

Not long after that afternoon, Tim gave me a CD with a selection of the day's jams. I asked him point-blank if the slow blues jam from late in the day was one of the tracks. He knew exactly which song I was talking about. He couldn't possibly know how much influence the song would have over me.

I don't know exactly when I got the idea for "Midnight Blue." I know I got the basic premise for the story while listening to "Let Me Hold You." I was probably driving, getting lost in the sentiment of the tune, and asking that dangerous question writers tend to ask: What If?

When I was a kid — maybe six or seven years old — my mom told me a story about a local deejay (it was the early 80's and they were still called deejays) who talked a caller out of committing suicide. That memory lay dormant in my mind for about twenty-five years, until I was thinking about how to create a story around this captivating blues song that no one, save for a few tanked smokers at The Toad House, had ever heard.

Give the song a listen. I think you'll agree that it was a good thing there was someone with the sense to push record the day four cats wandered into the Toad House on a Sunday afternoon.

They say, "the blues occurs when a negro is sad." Listening to "Let Me Hold You" is like taking in a lifetime of strife in a single take.

You can hear "Let Me Hold You" at www.theonlyfredsmith.com/single-post/2016/04/06/The-Greatest-Blues-Song-Youve-Never-Heard

If you're into the blues, it's worth it.

Larissa's Friday Night Earthquake

In 1992, singer-songwriter Tori Amos released her debut album, *Little Earthquakes*.

If a more empowering female soundtrack has ever been recorded, I'd like to hear it. I've got a hunch this album has gotten more broken-hearted women back on their feet than any collection of songs in history (or at least the 1990s. They don't yet keep data on heartaches overcome. If they did, I'd quote stats).

Little Earthquakes helped Larissa and guided her journey from shut-in to dancing queen. Funny how the right lyric can seem like it was written just for you when you see the world with a trampled heart.

I knew it wouldn't be apparent to every reader when I carefully sprinkled lyrics from each song on the album into the story. But if you've been where Larissa was and needed *Little Earthquakes* to shake free, you might have smiled when you caught the downstream current.

Buy Here, Pay Here

This story is about a young salesman with a gift for helping people go down an easy path they're already inclined to take. The more he succeeds, the farther out of poverty's grip he ascends. Of course, it's a zero-sum game. If he wins, someone else has to lose and descend into a typically unbreakable cycle of debt. He didn't invent the game. He was recruited to play it by someone earning override. There's always someone above the dirty deed who's taking a cut.

Much of our nation's urban economy is set up like the one in this story, legal businesses where desperation meets capitalism—and you can bet the deed to the place that there's someone above the carnage who's taking a hefty cut. There always is.

Cracked

We're not ourselves when we think we're being cheated on. The morals we rely on to stay in line with society's expectations tend to get suffocated by a more sinister voice that says the things we really want to hear—no matter how perverse.

Bad things happen when we succumb to the voice. Heavy drinking seldom leads to better decisions.

Over the years I've had a lot of friends give in to the voice while in the throes of a failing marriage. None cracked as bad as Mel.

It happens every day, though. Someone somewhere crosses the line, fueled by betrayal and alcohol. The newspapers don't always make the connection, but it's there. It's aways there.

One more thing, concerning language: Mel's inner voice freely uses the "c" word (the vile one that rhymes with runt) in a way that taunts Mel into action. I cringed every time I typed this word, it being (nearly) on par with the "n" word in its vileness.

I wrote a version of this story in which I omitted the "c" word, replacing it with a trio of poignant labels like "bitch," "slut," and "whore." I was more comfortable with this less-offensive version of the story, which is why I changed it back.

What good is the voice if it doesn't make you cringe?

The Exalted Cyclops

The idea for this story came to me when I learned about lynching postcards, pictures taken of lynched victims to be kept as a souvenir and a reminder of racial superiority. Most of these pictures were taken in the late 19th and early 20th century when photography was in its infancy. Today these images are haunting reminders of truth. These killings happened. The people in these pictures made sure they happened.

Many of the stories in this collection are about people realizing they need to make a change. What got them to the present will take them down a similar path in the future, which they've learned from experience isn't necessarily where they want to go.

The reader (I'm hoping) applauds this change, recognizing the protagonist has learned from his mistakes and will adjust his ways.

"The Exalted Cyclops" is the exception.

When you write a story about a white supremacist, your character is usually relegated to a predictable fate. He *must* realize the error of his ways. Most readers won't accept any other course. The only choice for the author is to decide whether the hate-monger makes the change in prison or in the free world where his choice has the greatest chance to affect others following in his deplorable footsteps.

There's another choice, one seldom made by authors lest they get labeled a bigot—or worse, one who promotes racism by not chastising it. The aging white supremacist can look back at his life, realize how everything he's done has lead him to the present, and decide he was wrong—not in doing what he did, but for not being radical enough in his terrorism.

I chose to take an uncompromising path with this story, one I knew wouldn't sit well with all readers. You don't have to like it, and it definitely shouldn't make you feel good.

I took the story where I did because the truly wicked seldom change course.

Your Trusted Reader

I had an idea for a story about two characters who have a passionate affair *through* the written word. The letter is their discrete rendezvous.

I thought about telling the story through a spate of texts, revealing only at the conclusion that at least one of the characters was in her 80s. The clunkiness of the exchange would be charming, I thought. Two experienced lovers fumbling like teenage virgins in a confusing new medium.

Charlotte and Gerald love the written word. They're lifelong prose-junkies. Language turns them on. Once I realized that, texting was out, replaced by lost art of letter writing.

The text message stifles expression. Sexting (text + sex) is like getting it on in the back seat of your parents' car. Exciting if the whole experience is new to you but limiting in the amount of creativity you can use if you've been around the block.

These two lovers needed a theatrical space for their affair. Emojis had no place.

Pencil Fight Club

The shard-in-the-eye incident never actually happened, despite my elementary school teachers' incessant warnings. I wish, however, the real "One-Lick Eddie" could have suffered a defeat like the one in the story.

But life isn't that perfect. Most of the time you just end up in detention.

Sammy Wilson's Last Christmas

A few years ago I spent some time in the oncology ward of a children's hospital. It was a place of unrequited hope.

Many of the kids in that ward would beat cancer and go on to lead amazing lives—but some didn't.

I wanted to give the place a miracle. Not just any miracle, a Christmas miracle…because that kind of hope has staying power.

By the way, notice anything unconventional about the real Santa? Sammy did. That's how he knew Santa was the real deal.

The Closet

I wrote "The Closet" in early 2012 and was considering adapting it into a film when tragedy struck in Newtown, Connecticut at Sandy Hook Elementary School on December 14, 2012. 26 people—20 of them children—lost their lives that day in a school shooting that nearly eight years later has become too familiar in America.

For a time, I considered burying the story on my hard drive, where it would live in unpublished anonymity.

As I write this, the massacre at Marjorie Stoneman Douglas High School in Parkland, Florida is less than one month old. My daughter is in the second grade. She and her classmates rehearse school shooting scenarios as often as they conduct fire drills.

By the time you read this, the next school shootings in America will have already happened. I can't stop them, but I felt it was important to tell a story about the real victims of school shootings—those who perish senselessly, and those who survive and must make sense of the chaos for the rest of their lives.

Nebraska Avenue

My wife and I called southeast Seminole Heights home for nine years from 2005 until 2014. We started our family there. Our daughter took her first steps in a house we owned off Nebraska Avenue, in a diverse neighborhood of hardworking families who knew each other's names.

It was while living in that old neighborhood that I wrote a short story about a teenage girl who walks down Tampa's infamous avenue to visit a distant cousin. There's a moral to the story. Sometimes, a neighborhood with a notorious reputation looks different when you experience it on foot as opposed to the comfort of your locked car.

I published a book of short stories called *How Long Can a White Girl Last on Nebraska Avenue? and other stories of wayward youth* in 2014.

Three years later, four people were murdered in my old neighborhood, innocent victims of a lunatic gunman the media would dub The Seminole Heights Killer.

Out of respect for the victims, their families, and the residents of Seminole Heights, I decided to pull *How Long Can a White Girl Last on Nebraska Avenue?* out of circulation. It's the right thing to do, but not because the book or this story had anything to do with the four tragedies that took place in my old neighborhood.

I pulled the book because while "Nebraska Avenue" paints a positive picture of an area that is still a great neighborhood full of interesting people, it's also a place that can't pretend to be innocent anymore.

About the author

Fred Smith is an author and filmmaker. His previous writings include *The Incident Last Tuesday,* a play, and *Invisible Innocence,* a nonfiction memoir of former homeless youth, Maria Fabian.

In college he played baseball with a future World Series MVP and played drums in a band that once opened for James Brown. Since then he's published a music magazine, made a feature film, installed his own sewer line, married the greatest woman on planet Earth, and become a dad.

Fred lives in Tampa, FL enjoying every second he can with his wife, Marie; daughter, Madison; and dog, Libby.

Visit theonlyfredsmith.com to learn more about his books, plays, and films and to hear him play the occasional drum solo.

Other books by Fred Smith:

Available on TheOnlyFredSmith.com and Amazon.com.

The Incident Last Tuesday
a play by Fred Smith

Four High School Students.
One Crime.
Someone has to pay.
Someone has to talk.

Lies, manipulation, and deception run rampant during an afternoon interrogation hellbent on discovering who is the expendable culprit.

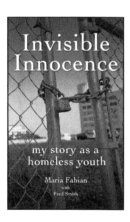

Invisible Innocence:
my story as a homeless youth
by Maria Fabian with Fred Smith

This is the story of a homeless youth told through the eyes of a trampled soul who found the courage to believe and the strength to come forward so others may finally understand a problem our society can no longer ignore.

Films by Fred Smith

available to stream at TheOnlyFredSmith.com

"The Closet"

A short film by Fred Smith

Two strangers rely on each other for sanity and survival while hiding out in in a janitor's closet during a school shooting.

"The Kids in the Shadows:

stories from homeless youth"

A documentary by Fred Smith

These are the stories of the kids we've let slip through society's cracks.

TheOnlyFredSmith.com

Visit Fred's site and sign up to his blog
'A Crack in the Room Tone'
to receive his latest stories, movies, and occasional drum solos.

Made in the USA
Coppell, TX
22 May 2020